THE WOLF'S VIXEN

SAMANTHA ALLARD

Copyright © 2022, Samantha Allard

Cover Art © 2022 Dreams2Media

An EveL Worlds Production : www.worlds.EveLanglais.com

ALL RIGHTS RESERVED

This story is a work of fiction and the characters, events and dialogue found within the story are of the author's imagination and are not to be construed as real. Any resemblance to actual events or persons, either living or deceased, is completely coincidental.

No part of this book may be reproduced or shared in any form or by any means, electronic or mechanical, including but not limited to digital copying, file sharing, audio recording, email and printing without permission in writing from the author.

ACKNOWLEDGMENTS

Having the opportunity to write in Eve Langlais has been a great deal of fun. I want to thank her for opening this world up for fellow writers to build and expand. I've been a fan of her work since Kodiak Point. I also want to thank Jess Renee Ripley for doing a wonderful job at editing and leaving inspiring comments to spur me on.

And finally, to Rebecca Poole, who did an excellent job on the cover art.

For fans old and new. Welcome to Neil and Lizzie's story.

CHAPTER ONE

Elizabeth "Lizzie" Adams lived by a set of strict rules:

Never steal from someone who couldn't afford the loss.

Make sure her targets deserved it.

Always keep her identity a well-guarded secret.

Working with a third party, someone she'd never met who helped her keep her online footprint well hidden, had been worth every penny. It was the only reason she dodged all those seeking revenge. If anyone had found out who she was, they would have killed her long ago.

All she needed to do was take Elijah's memory stick from his safe and drop it off at the designated point. After the client picked it up, they would transfer her fee to one of her offshore accounts. Nice and clean. The way she liked all her jobs.

She moved through the nearly deserted building in her fox form, noting the gentle hum of activity. The daytime security team was swapping out with the night shift, which had been her way in. The teams each consisted of four guys who wouldn't have looked out of place on a rugby field and might prove to be a problem if they found her. Elijah had hired the best to protect his valuable assets.

Luckily, nobody noticed her slip into the building and head toward her prize, which was kept in the office safe on the top floor. She'd taken the time to memorize the layout of the building. The floors were like a labyrinth; a couple of wrong turns and she would be in a world of trouble.

It would have been easier to take the lift, but many things could go wrong with that route. Too many chances for Lizzie to be caught by the men with guns. That left the staircase.

Six flights would feel like she'd tried to climb a mountain, but first, she needed to get through the locked door that led to them.

When she'd disguised herself as a cleaner and visited the location earlier, she'd discovered a hiding place, which she now darted toward. The table next to the door was large enough for her to hide under. Even better, if she pressed against the farthest wall and kept still, her camouflage would kick in.

She wasn't sure where she had gained the ability to blend into her surroundings. Lizzie's shifter form was a fennec fox, a cute animal with large ears and humongous eyes but without a natural form of disguise. She'd always wondered if maybe she had chameleon somewhere in her family tree.

Not that her fox form alone wasn't good for sneaking around. Being small meant she could slink in and out of places without anyone noticing her. Human guards, without the concept of the supernatural world, wouldn't be looking for a four-legged thief. She liked a challenge, but sometimes an easy job was a nice change of pace.

When she skidded underneath the table, she slipped into the natural blind spot and kept her eyes on the door in front of her. Her window of opportunity was short and risky. If she fucked up, the job would be over before it had begun.

There was a click as the door opened, and a guard dressed in a smart black suit came into view. He raised the radio to his mouth. "All five floors have been checked. We've got one worker on the third floor, but they'll be out in an hour."

There was a garbled response. "Have you ordered the pizzas yet?"

Lizzie dashed forward as the guard started to saunter away, his back facing the closing door. She made it inside the stairwell just before the door clicked shut behind her.

Her tiny heart raced. If she'd been a more standard version of the adorable creature, she would have had a heart attack long ago.

If the guard decided to pass on the pizza and return to his post, it left Lizzie only a few minutes. She looked up and around to identify a few places she could hide if she needed to. If Tall, Dark, and Ugly reappeared when she was on the stairs, he'd see her. Lizzie counted to ten, threw a silent prayer to any god who took pity on thieves, and cursed whoever invented stairs.

It was one thing to have incredible strength and endurance, but nobody liked a prolonged cardio workout. Especially considering that her tiny legs needed to carry her own body and the small pouch that hung around her neck. It would be near impossible to complete the job without it. She knew what her limits were, and there was no way she could get into the secure door to Elijah's office without the right tools. The office could only be accessed with a four-digit number and a fingerprint. One of those couldn't be hacked.

Arriving at her destination, she crouched by the keypad, and the change swept over her. One minute she was a cute fox with fathomless black eyes; the next, she was a naked woman. She had no problem with a bit of nudity if ignoring it helped her get the job done. Thanks to the blueprints of the building, she knew there weren't any cameras on this floor. The people Elijah worked for didn't like being caught on film.

She stood and stretched, shaking her head. Her stark white hair brushed against her shoulders as she tugged on the pouch around her neck. It opened, and she pulled out a small glass strip, two thin panes pressed together. With care, she pulled them apart and unpeeled the thumb-sized mold protected between them. When it was secure over her thumb, she pressed it against the scanner.

Green light.

The four-digit code was the problem. Security changed the numbers every day. There were three chances before the silent alarm was triggered. She closed her eyes. She tilted her head from side to side, breathing deeply, and shook her hands. When she was ready, she opened her eyes and tapped in the number. If she got it wrong, the light would turn red.

Red.

Shit.

She rolled her head from side to side. Something clicked at the base of her skull, and some of the tension left her. She wasn't some wet-behind-the-ears rookie. The unfortunate truth was that if she got this one wrong, the job needed to be put off for another day. She had a flawless reputation. Failure wasn't an option.

She pressed her counterfeit thumbprint against the keypad again and typed in the number.

Green.

She fought against the urge to do a happy dance. It could wait until she returned to her apartment and got into some clothes. She nudged the door open and peeked around. A large bookcase encompassed the left wall, and there was a door on the right, which led to some filing cabinets. They held valuable information in them, but they weren't her target.

She made her way to the painting behind the desk. As she made out faint details in the near darkness, she pulled a pair of gloves from her pouch and slipped them on. She ran the tips of her fingers across the frame until she found the ridge—a hidden button— and pressed it.

The painting swung off the wall like a door opening. Many people liked safes that came with plenty of security features. Those weren't easy to crack. Elijah, on the other hand, wanted things old school. That made Lizzie's job easier. She flexed her fingers and tucked her hair behind her ears.

Whoever designed safes hadn't considered that a shifter would be the ones who cracked them. She closed her eyes and pressed her ear against the steel. Then she got to work, her fingers on the dial. She'd spent months honing her skills, and so far, her record was three minutes. Every click was a welcomed sound and proof that the decision to learn had been time well spent.

With the last click, she opened the safe. Her eyes had adjusted to the darkness, and she pulled out a small stack of papers. Resting on top was the flash drive. *Jackpot!*

She placed it into her pouch, replaced the stack of papers, closed the safe, and returned the painting to its original position.

Then she removed the gloves and returned them to her pouch, checking it one last time before she shifted back into her fox form and waited.

The door opened.

Just on time.

The man was a black silhouette, a gun in his hand. He was human. It would take his eyes a while to adjust to the darkness. He scanned the area as Lizzie waited for her opportunity to dart past him through the door he'd so thoughtfully opened for her. He moved purposefully, keeping his gun pointed as he swept the room.

She didn't stay and wait for him to turn around. She heard him radio in as she slipped through the closing door and scrambled for cover under the receptionist's desk. "You better put a call out to the tech guys. I don't know what triggered the alarm, but there's nobody up here."

A garbled response.

"I don't know what to tell you; there's nobody up here. You're more than welcome to check if you don't believe me."

Escape. The animal part of her brain threatened to overtake her human half.

No, we need to give it a few minutes, and then we'll go. I promise we'll get out of here.

Scared.

No, we're not. We've done the job we've been hired to do, and we've done it well. We've never failed, and we aren't going to start now. You trust me, don't you?

Trust? There was a pause like her fox was taking the time to consider the word. *Yes.*

Then relax; we'll be back home before you know it.

LIZZIE CLIMBED UP THE FIRE ESCAPE AND THROUGH THE window into her apartment. She shifted back into her human form and picked up the robe she left draped over the back of the couch, keeping the pouch around her neck. She didn't plan on letting it out of her sight until she dropped it off at the train station in locker number 1408 for pickup.

"Hello, Miss Adams."

The unexpected sound made her jump. She spun around and noticed she wasn't alone. A man sat in the shadows.

The apartment was her inner sanctum. It was under a different name, and there wasn't anything that linked it to her. She never invited anyone there, and knowing someone else was there made her skin crawl. So how did this man get in? How did he know her name? "Who are you?"

"That's not important. I have a job for you."

"I think I'll pass."

There was a soft chuckle. "It's cute you think you have a choice. Have a read of the folder when you wake up."

"What do you mean, wake up?" A thick arm snaked around her waist in a blur of movement, and there was a sharp pain in her neck. Her vision started to become cloudy. Whatever they had hit her with, it was potent stuff.

"Who are you?" She tried to push the words past her lips one more time.

"Call me The Broker. There's a burner phone in the folder. We'll be in contact."

Lizzie slumped to the floor, and the darkness swallowed her whole.

CHAPTER TWO

Neil Yun tapped the bar counter while waiting for his contact to arrive. The Dirty Habit wasn't busy, but Neil was a frequent enough patron that he knew the customers would start to roll in, in a couple of hours. He wanted to be back on the plane by then. He promised Jackson he'd visit the old stomping grounds.

Soft jazz played over the speakers. The classy interior of The Dirty Habit didn't match the odd name choice. It sounded like a place that could be discovered down some dark alleyway. Somewhere to disappear in a haze of alcohol and drugs. A hundred years or so ago, it *was* that kind of establishment, but The Dirty Habit's current owners had kept the name as a homage to days gone by, even though they'd classed up the joint.

Neil glanced outside. He didn't know when it started to rain, but the windows were now slick with raindrops, and the people on the sidewalks rushed by. Some had umbrellas, but others must have missed the forecast this morning, as they attempted to keep dry under folded newspapers.

"You want another drink?"

"Please." Neil raised his whisky glass. The amber liquid sloshed in the bottom, diluted by a few ice cubes.

"Coming right up." The bartender was pretty, with onyx hair and bright sapphire eyes. She wore a short skirt, which rode up whenever she moved. Every time it did, she tugged it back down. The whole look was completed with a form-fitted white blouse, a thin black tie, and a matching waistcoat.

Neil didn't usually drink on the job, but he hardly considered a meeting with Gerald Alberty work. They'd known each other for years and were friends, even if all their encounters ended with an exchange of money for the information Gerald gave him.

The bartender smiled as she pushed his refilled drink toward him. Neil opened his wallet and pulled out a twenty. "Keep the change."

"Thank you." She nodded toward the door before asking, "Is that whom you're waiting for?"

Neil glanced at the mirror above the bar. "That would be him. Glass of whatever you have on tap, please."

The woman nodded and started to prepare Gerald's drink.

Gerald was in his fifties but could pass for someone in his thirties thanks to his shifter genes. He wore his hair long and in a tight braid down his back. Neil noticed how people looked at him as he walked past. Gerald scanned the bar until he saw Neil.

By the time he reached the counter, his drink was ready. He sat as Neil paid the bartender.

"Have you been waiting long?"

"I got into the city a few hours ago."

"You should have said. I could have met you sooner." Gerald pulled out his phone, pressed a few buttons, and replaced it in the inside pocket of his deep brown suit jacket. Neil did the same, opening the Bluetooth and linking his phone with Gerald's.

"Don't worry about it. How's the family?"

They spent a few minutes talking about Gerald's harem. In Gerald's breed of horse shifters, males were rare, and they were expected to take several lovers in the hope that one or more would become pregnant. He often joked it was dirty work but somebody had to do it. It would have sounded flippant to anyone else, but Neil knew Gerald loved his three wives.

Neil's phone vibrated against his chest, and he pulled it out, closed the Bluetooth connection, and transferred money across to Gerald. They looked like two friends catching up to anyone else who watched them. The Dirty Habit had a human clientele. It didn't mean the bad guys didn't or wouldn't use humans. The supernatural world was a secret, and there were rules to ensure it stayed that way. The thing was the bad guys didn't follow the rules.

"How's your love life? The last time we talked, you were dating Florence from your department, weren't you?"

Neil shrugged as he downed the contents of his glass. "She found her mate. It wasn't me." That was the downside of dating shifters; so many of them were the type who had their destined mate. At least Neil and Florence had an understanding. Whatever happened between two consenting, non-mated adults was just a bit of fun. There weren't supposed to be any hard feelings when the mating bond kicked in with someone else. Even if Neil knew and understood, the truth still stung. "It's fine."

"It isn't judging by the look on your face." The horse shifter took a deep drink from his glass. "You travel all over the world for work. You'll find her."

"We do a lot of dangerous work. Maybe it's a good thing I haven't met her yet." He stood and redid the button on his suit jacket. The information Gerald brought had been downloaded to Neil's phone and then sent off to the secure servers at Neil's FUC office. He hoped it would provide a lead in the cases surrounding the thefts and attempted thefts of books by Miklos Bathory, a Hungarian philosopher who'd been alive during the medieval era. While most of his books were written in code, they held the first mentions of the *Isten Teremtmenyei*. The creatures of God. Shifters.

The shifter secret had been safe throughout history, but if Bathory's books ended up in the wrong hands, it could mean the end of it.

The Furry United Coalition worked to keep the shifter world safe and secure. That was precisely what Neil was trying to do.

"The world is always going to be dangerous. It's the nature of the job."

"Very true." Neil shrugged. He had more important things to think about than dating. Not even the pretty bartender piqued his interest. Not when he was on a critical mission. "Thanks for the information. We'll be in touch."

He would have liked to stay longer but had a plane to catch.

———

A COUPLE OF HOURS LATER, NEIL WAS ON A PLANE WAITING for it to take off. He hated flying. His inner animal, a wolf, hated it more. The upside was that FUC footed the bill for first class. The flight attendant, a man in a bright red suit, walked down the aisle and talked to the passengers. Neil checked his watch. They should have taken off five minutes ago. Nobody had started to grumble, but he knew it was just a matter of time. People rioted over much less.

Neil's inner wolf threatened as much, as both he and the animal shared a dislike of flying. It would take fifteen hours to get to Vancouver and then an hour or so needed to get to Nonamesville. The small town was in the middle of nowhere and played host to the Furry United Coalition Newbie Academy, where his friend Jackson lived with his mate, a mouse shifter called Aubrey. Well, not at the actual Academy but close to it.

Extra time stuck on the tarmac only added to the time it would take before Neil could get back to work.

He crossed his arms and stretched out his legs, enjoying his comfortable seat and a cold drink and trying to convince his wolf that they'd be taking off soon enough.

"What's taking so long?" Neil asked the flight attendant when he passed again.

"We're just waiting for a passenger."

"I didn't think you guys waited around for people."

The attendant shrugged. "It's above my pay grade, I'm afraid." He continued his walk down the aisle and updated the other travelers.

Neil took a deep breath and sighed. His wolf paced inside of him. *It's okay, buddy. We'll be taking off soon.*

The wolf suddenly went silent as a scent hit Neil with all the impact of a punch. He raised himself in his chair to better look at the person who had stunned his wolf.

Hushed whispers came from behind him as the woman came into view. For a split second, Neil forgot how to breathe. She was stunning. Her hair was white, held a slight curl, and came to her shoulders. Her lips were painted a dark red. On most, the color would have looked harsh, but this woman resembled a badass porcelain doll. Neil couldn't take his eyes away from her.

She walked closer to him, checking her ticket and looking up at the numbers above each row of seats, trying to find her spot. A few people glared at her, but she either didn't notice or care.

She stopped next to Neil, looked up from her ticket, and then down at the empty window seat next to him. She shrugged off her bag and put that and her jacket in the overhead compartment.

It took a moment for something to click.

This captivating woman was his seatmate for their extended flight.

He was a seasoned agent, and he'd never been rendered speechless before.

When he stood from his seat and stepped into the aisle to let her pass, her eyes widened in surprise. She quickly recovered, and her expression returned to indifference.

He pondered over her scent as he retook his seat. He couldn't figure out what animal she was, but she was undoubtedly some kind of shifter.

They both listened, and the flight attendant went through their script. Neil tried to turn his attention back to the newspaper he'd bought from the kiosk. He'd been staring at the stranger like a kid with a crush, and while it had been a nice distraction, it wasn't enough to shake the impending feeling of doom he always got when he was about to fly.

His hands were in tight fists, and as the plane started to move, he jumped. His paper tore, and the woman made a noise of surprise.

"Are you okay?"

Her husky voice shot right down to his groin. He dropped the paper into his lap, hiding the erection, which appeared with such speed it left him dizzy.

"I hate being up in the air."

The whole situation was ridiculous. He had survived too many dangerous encounters to count and had been fine. What was it about flying that scared him so much?

She turned in her chair, and for a moment, Neil thought she would touch him. His wolf liked the idea a lot.

"Do you want to hear my theory?"

The plane continued down the runway. He needed

something, anything, to take his mind off what was about to happen. He nodded, not trusting himself to speak.

"It's all about giving up control for our kind. For the ones who spend most of their lives on the ground, there's a certainty to being earthbound. Flying? It's not natural unless you sprout feathers."

The plane shuddered, and Neil grabbed the armrest. His animal was close to the surface. It wanted out. The mysterious woman leaned closer, and her lips brushed the curve of his ear. "I imagine you don't like giving up control," she purred. "To put your life into someone else's hands. Sometimes that's all I ever want to do. In my line of work, it's hard to put your trust in anyone else. I envy people who can give up their hard-won control." If it was possible, Neil became even harder. "For them to surrender completely."

After the plane took off and the steward said they could undo their belts, Neil turned to face her. She smiled, her face half hidden by the magazine she read. The look in her amber eyes was mischievous. She winked before she leaned back into her chair and lowered her reading material. "Did I help?"

"Help what?"

"Take your mind off of it?"

Neil collapsed back into his chair. "I think you did a lot more than that."

CHAPTER THREE

THE MAN DIDN'T SAY ANYTHING ELSE TO HER, AND SHE tried to get some sleep. Talking to him was a nice distraction, but that was all it was: a distraction to take her mind off the fact she was fucked.

When she woke up that morning, her head felt two sizes too small for her brain. Whatever they had injected her with left her with the worst possible hangover. She didn't know how they'd found her, and her first instinct had been to run as far and as fast as she could. Then she saw the folder. The one they had left for her.

Curious, she had sat and flipped through it. Details of the job had been on the first page, and that had been enough for her to put it in the bin. Whoever wanted to hire her had a few vital screws loose. Nobody robbed that Academy. It was a suicide mission. That was when the photo had fallen out—the one of Amanda.

Scrawled on the bottom of it, in thick black ink, were the words: *We know where she is.*

Lizzie hadn't spoken to her adopted and very human

sister in years. The last time they had seen each other, at their mother's funeral, they had argued. Amanda had gone into law, and Lizzie was a thief, not to mention she had to keep her shifter side secret from her sister. It was safe to say they didn't have much in common.

Yet someone had threatened Amanda because of Lizzie.

The thought made Lizzie's stomach twist up into knots. She had been careful; she even went by a different surname. There shouldn't have been anything connecting them. How had they known?

They hadn't come out and said it, but the message was clear. Either Lizzie took the job or her sister would pay the price. They weren't even asking her to do it for free. They were paying her, half on accepting the job and the other when it was completed.

That was a consolation, she supposed.

Lizzie spent the day memorizing the layout and booking a seat on a plane to Canada. The best she could come up with was one sliver of a chance to complete the job, to get in and out without anyone discovering her identity.

But it would be tough. More challenging than any other job she'd ever done. There were reasons she never stole from shifters. Not only were they aware of shifters, so they'd spot an out-of-place fox a mile away, but they had heightened senses and enhanced strength that made them formidable opponents.

She didn't know how many trainees were at the Academy, but she'd undoubtedly be outnumbered.

Then there were the more practical matters of doing a

job so many time zones out of her usual one. The time difference was going to be a real bitch to get her head around. British Columbia, Canada, was about seven hours behind.

Lizzie peeked at the man next to her. He was handsome, with a strong jaw and intense eyes. He had been cute in his panicked state, but now he was relaxed or close to it. It looked like he was reading, but Lizzie noticed his eyes weren't moving. It was like he was trying to stare a hole into the paper.

"You feel any better?" she asked.

The corner of his mouth kicked up into a smile. "Just trying to figure out if I should die of embarrassment."

Lizzie shifted in her seat, turning her body toward him to continue watching him. "And why's that? I would say you're only human, but we both know that's not true. I'm Lizzie, by the way."

"Neil." He offered his hand, which she shook. The moment they touched, a spark of awareness shot through her, and she pulled away from him in shock. *What was that?*

Though she was stunned, Neil's expression hadn't changed. Hadn't he felt it, too, whatever it was?

"You're going to Vancouver?" he asked.

She nodded. It wasn't easy to get to the FUCN'A since it wasn't on any map. The information she found in the file suggested that the Academy was in British Columbia, in the Rocky Mountains. Then she would need to rent a car and stake out the area, hoping to spot a shifter who looked like an agent and then follow them to see if they'd lead her to the hidden school.

"I'm heading there as well."

A thought occurred to her. She was looking for a shifter in BC, and here was a shifter right next to her, headed right there. She took a chance, fishing for information. "I've always wanted to see the Academy. Got some time off work. Thought I'd go and have a look." She didn't have much experience with shifters but knew it was difficult to lie to one. With heightened senses, someone like her could read someone with surprising accuracy. She would need to tell the truth or something close to it.

"Is Alyce trying to recruit you for a teaching job?" he asked as some of the tension left him.

"I'm going there for some kind of job," she murmured, bending the truth again.

"Good luck." He chuckled. "Alyce Cooper is a heck of a director. From what I hear, she always gets what she wants."

Lizzie nodded. Great. Another reminder of the FUC competence. "So what about you?"

"I don't work there, no. One of my friends lives around the Academy, though. He's settled down there recently with his mate."

She couldn't detect a lie. The honesty practically radiated off him—the quintessential good guy. Lizzie hadn't met many of those in her line of work. It was refreshing.

She took another chance. "How are you planning on getting there?"

"I left my car at the car park. Do you need a lift?" He faced her, and she got a much better look that led to a shiver running through her. She had no idea how far

FUCN'A was from the Vancouver airport. She should be focusing on the job, making plans and backup strategies. Neil was much too handsome. A terrible distraction.

But what was the alternative? Spending time trying to follow a random shifter who may or may not be heading to the Academy?

She rubbed her lower lip with her little finger, not minding she smudged her lipstick. "How do I know you're not some serial killer who will murder me on the drive there?"

"That's easy." He reached over and took her hand, and another shot of awareness hit her. She didn't pull away from him, but she did make a mental note that her fox liked to be touched by him as well. He placed her hand on his hard chest. "I promise I'm not some serial killer hoping to get you alone."

"Your heart's racing a little."

His cheeks reddened slightly. The sight was adorable. "That's because I've got a pretty lady sitting next to me who has me thinking a lot of interesting things. Nothing to do with murdering her. Scout's honor."

She moved away and found a comfortable position in her seat. She believed him. The real problem was the attraction she felt for him. For the first time in a long time, she was in complete agreement with her fox on wanting a man. That was rare. For the longest time, her animal hadn't shown interest in anyone. It was for that reason she shouldn't get involved with him.

That didn't mean they couldn't travel together, however. Flirting could make the trip go by faster.

"I'll travel with you then. That's all I want, though.

Don't get any funny ideas that this will lead anywhere." Before he could respond, she added a decided, "I'm going to get some sleep."

As she closed her eyes, he moved closer to her. He mirrored her move from earlier, with his mouth close to her ear. "I like to think I'm a gentleman, but we both know you don't believe what you just said."

Lizzie shivered but didn't open her eyes. "That's very presumptuous of you."

"Not presumptuous. I just believe in honesty."

She listened as he moved around to get comfortable in his seat. There was plenty of space in first class that their arms didn't even brush against each other, much to her disappointment. That would have been better. She liked touching him, and it had put her into a state of hyperawareness that meant it wouldn't be easy to fall asleep.

Instead of focusing on the sexy shifter Neil, Lizzie thought about Amanda. They'd left her a burner phone and indicated that they'd send a file to it in two weeks. It would give her a new identity and access to the bank account they'd locked her out of. The one Lizzie had been squirreling money into.

She had to think about the results of succeeding in the mission because she definitely couldn't think about what might happen if she failed. What might they do to Amanda if Lizzie failed?

That wasn't a risk she was willing to take.

Lizzie woke to someone nudging her in the ribs. "That better be your elbow," she muttered underneath her breath as she opened her eyes. One of the flight attendants had stopped next to her with a tray filled with breakfast sandwiches and a pot of fresh coffee.

Neil chuckled. "I didn't think you wanted to miss the coffee trolley. You're British, right? Do you want tea?"

She frowned at him. "Would you like to keep breathing?" She smiled at the server. "Coffee, black with three sugars. Thanks."

"Milky coffee, two sugars," Neil requested.

She dug right into the sandwich, unable to remember the last time she ate something. She usually went home after a job and feasted since shifting from animal to human was hell on the system and required extra calories. But she'd been drugged and then so focused on getting ready for the job that she'd not had a chance to prepare herself any meals.

When she finished eating, she noticed Neil was watching her. She brushed some crumbs from her lower lip. "What?"

He shrugged before he turned his attention back to his own food. His eyes were black. Where had his mind drifted to? "Where are you from in the UK?"

"Norfolk. I've got a flat in London for work." She didn't want to get into too many details about herself. "How about you? What are you doing so far away from home?"

"I travel for work. I had to meet a client in London."

"Were you there long?"

"No. It was a quick business trip. Wasn't much time for sightseeing."

She sipped her drink. "What do you do?"

"I'm in communications. What about you?"

"Acquisitions."

"You like it?"

"I do." Lizzie held up her empty cup, catching the flight attendant's attention. The man nodded and hurried over to provide a refill.

"It's always good to do something you're passionate about," Neil said once the flight attendant left.

"Why do you say that?"

He smiled, and her breath caught. For the love of God, he needed to come with a warning label stamped across his forehead. *Keep away, ladies. This man is a risk to your heart and your knickers.* "The way your eyes lit up when you said it."

Her face went hot. *Christ, am I blushing?* Desperate to take the spotlight off herself, she asked, "Do you enjoy *your* job?"

"Communications calls for a specific set of skills." He shrugged, but he looked more self-satisfied than nonchalant. "I'm good at what I do."

CHAPTER FOUR

They spent most of the trip making small talk. Neil hadn't met anyone like Lizzie before, and he'd met many. It was a bonus to traveling all over the world.

The problem was Lizzie stirred something inside him that he hadn't felt in a long time. Not since Florence, because he'd felt there hadn't been any need for it. His line of work was dangerous, and bringing someone into his life who didn't understand what he did was selfish. Even his wolf had been happy with the arrangement.

"You keep staring at me."

He blinked. "I do?" What had she been talking about? He couldn't remember. The curve of her red lips had led his mind to wander.

Lizzie studied him as she sipped her white wine. "How are you about landings?"

He went lightheaded. "Is it that time already?" Neil turned in his seat and looked out of the window. The sky had turned a darker shade of blue. At least he wouldn't be able to see the landing stripe rush up along the side of the plane.

"We've got half an hour. The flight attendants are starting to go through their landing procedures."

His heart started to race, and as he was about to close his eyes, Lizzie reached out to him. He looked at their joined hands then back at her.

"You're going to be fine, Neil. I want you to focus on my touch." She traced a pattern with the pad of her thumb. "Can you do that for me?"

He nodded.

"Good boy," she purred.

"You know that's not fair."

"What isn't?"

His heart was now racing for a different reason. "You know the effect you're having on me. There's no way you can't tell." His cock was hard. If all his blood kept rushing in that direction, he was going to start seeing stars.

She lifted her eyebrow. "I'm just helping take your mind off what's about to happen. I'm being a good travel buddy. Now shush, the flight attendant is talking."

Neil had traveled on enough planes that he knew the speech by heart. It never made it any easier to accept. Lizzie helped in her way, leaning against him. The way her breasts pressed against his arm had to be deliberate. So was the way she ran her free hand up and down the length of his arm.

His wolf howled in frustration. He wanted her as much as his next breath. *I feel your pain, buddy.* She had done a decent job of chasing away his anxieties, but stroking his arm had him thinking of her stroking something else.

"How are you feeling?"

"Horny and terrified. It's an odd combination." He reached out and touched her thigh. She shivered as he brushed his fingertips against her leg.

"Does touching help?"

"Do you want me to stop?"

They were playing a dangerous game. Already moving past flirting and on to touching when they had a long road trip ahead of them and she had said she didn't want anything more than to travel with him. He was walking a fine line, and while he didn't want to stop, he would if she told him to.

Even so, her smile was mischievous. She took his paper from where he'd stashed it and opened it, using the paper to cover her lap.

"No."

They were on a plane, and while there were many people, it was dark and no one was paying attention to them. He couldn't resist the invitation to tease her.

He ran his fingers up her thigh and back to her knee. It was an odd angle, and as if she read his mind, she adjusted in her seat to be closer to him and parted her legs.

"Do you like me touching you?" he whispered, trusting her sensitive ears would hear him.

She nodded. "More than I should."

"Do you know how hard you made me?" She shook her head. "I could break rocks with this thing."

He looked around; everyone else was in their seats. He

raised his hand and cupped her through the fabric of her jeans. "You're so hot down there. Are you wet for me?"

"This is insane," she hissed. "I've never done this before."

"Me neither," he admitted. "You feel it too, don't you?"

"Like my animal is trying to claw out of my skin?"

The atmosphere in the cabin changed. They had begun their descent. Neil focused on teasing her and not on what was going on with the plane. "Have you been with a shifter before?"

"No, I haven't even been around many." She shook her head. "I was brought up by humans."

That was it. A blinding need because it had been such a long time? His wolf was urging him on. It was maddening.

Bite. Claim. Ours.

Neil leaned closer. Lizzie had closed her eyes, lost in the moment. "Do you know what we should do when we land?"

She looked at him with warm auburn eyes, her animal close to the surface as she ground against his hand. "Find the nearest motel and fuck this tension away?"

Neither one of them turned on the light as the hotel room door swung shut behind them. She stepped in before him, and from behind her, Neil helped her take off her jacket. As soon as her skin was exposed, he ran his hands up her arms, absorbing the feel of her against his fingertips. She was spectacular, and he couldn't wait a moment longer to have her.

He pulled her hair over her shoulder and brushed a kiss against the curve of her neck. She shivered against him. He tugged at the bottom of her T-shirt before he pulled it over her head. The moment the fabric was gone, she spun in his arms, looking up at him with black eyes.

"You're beautiful." He licked his lips when he looked down at her breasts.

She loosened his tie and discarded it on the floor. Then she set to work unbuttoning his shirt. "Your clothes are more complicated than mine."

"I did pack more clothes." That was all she needed to hear. She tugged at the shirt, and the buttons popped, landing somewhere on the floor.

He lifted her, and she wrapped her legs around his waist. With one arm, he kept her in balance, and with the other, he pulled her closer, brushing his lips against hers, holding back from totally consuming her so they could enjoy the tease for just a moment longer.

She moaned, and he couldn't hold back any longer. He pressed her lips hard against hers and deepened the kiss while walking them toward the bed.

He didn't break contact with her, and with skilled fingers, he unbuttoned her jeans. She shimmied out of the constrictive clothes, and his body mourned the momentary separation of their bodies, though their mouths stayed together.

Her desire was thick in the air. His mouth watered at the thought of tasting her. He broke the kiss and moved from her bra-covered breasts, the curve of her stomach, and between her thighs. Her fingers ran through his hair, urging him lower.

"You want me to kiss you here?" He brushed his

fingers across the darkened fabric of her panties, which were wet with her desire. She was as turned on as he was.

"Is the sky blue?" The words left her on a moan, and he smiled.

He kissed the wet fabric and then quickly pulled them off her and discarded them, enveloping her sex in his mouth, lapping her with his tongue. She held him in place as he feasted on her. She cried out as he worked her clit with his tongue, and those cries gave way to moans as he pressed inside her with his fingers. She tasted as good, if not better, than he thought possible.

He looked up the line of her body, admiring the sexy way her nipples were half exposed in her bra and her arms were now above her head, gripping onto the headboard. She looked at him with hooded eyes, and something snapped into place for him.

Mate.

The random thought popped into his mind, and he paused.

"Don't stop! I'm so close!" she cried.

He pushed the thought to the back of his mind. He'd worry about that later. Right. That instant all he needed to do was focus on her. To get her off so hard that she saw stars.

He nibbled on the bundle of nerves, and she screamed. It wasn't one of pain. The evidence of her release coated his tongue, and he growled in satisfaction as she shuddered.

Bite. Claim. Mate.

She shoved him off the bed and followed him to the floor. The move was unexpected but not unwelcome. She fumbled with his trousers, freeing his cock. In one swift moment, she straddled him and he was inside of her.

"Holy fuck." Her warm heat was incredible. The whole experience held an intensity he had never experienced, and it was far from over.

She moved over him, bringing him pleasure in ways he didn't think possible.

And Lizzie was basically a stranger. The insanity of it all wasn't lost on him. He didn't know her other than the few snippets of information they had shared. She could have been anyone, and it didn't matter.

All that mattered was the need, which went to a deeper level.

Neil kissed her as the words that had been repeating in his mind moved to the forefront, coming to life inside of him. His wolf's voice was clear in his head.

Bite. Claim. Mate. She is ours.

He couldn't stand it any longer. He flipped her over so she was pinned under him as he took over thrusting and leading their momentum. Her happy moans proved that she wasn't upset with the position change. Neil kissed her neck and shoulder, trying to keep them soft, but as he came closer to climax, they became harder.

His heart raced. An ache had started in his jaw. The familiar sensation made his breath catch. His wolf was pushing to be free. Lizzie hadn't noticed, too caught up in her impending release. God, she was beautiful. He gritted his teeth and willed his wolf to calm down.

You don't want to hurt her.

She is ours!

It would be so easy to leave his mark on her, but he

had to hold back. *Enjoy the moment, have some fun, but don't do something stupid.*

Lizzie screamed his name, the sound a mixture of pain and pleasure. She went tight around him, and every thought of claiming her fled his mind.

His release hit him like a baseball bat to the back of the skull, harder than it had ever been before.

When he could see straight, she was watching his face, panting just as hard as he was.

He moved off her, pulling her into his arms while they lay curled up on the floor.

They'd both been traveling for fifteen hours, and he needed a shower, but that could wait for a little while. The urge to just hold her overrode everything else.

Mate.

CHAPTER FIVE

The last twenty-four hours, though, had made her question everything she'd ever thought about herself and her life.

Lizzie didn't make a habit of doing things she regretted. She wasn't an impulsive person. Everything was always well thought out. She took every eventuality into consideration before taking action. But now? A mysterious man threatened her sister, so Lizzie had taken on a job that might end up being impossible.

Then there was Neil, the shifter who now slept beside her in the hotel room bed, which they'd made it to after showering and going one more round.

Their night together had been completely out of character for her. But was it something she regretted?

She looked at him before brushing a strand of black hair off his forehead She got out of bed, not bothering with her clothes, and sat on the windowsill.

No, she didn't regret anything.

Yet.

They'd had a little bit of fun. That was all it was. It couldn't be any more than that. Neil had told her that the drive would be a few days, so perhaps it would be harmless to let the fun continue for that long.

For a short amount of time when she could pretend she was normal. Well, normal for a shifter. Then, Neil would go off to his friend's house, and she would go off to the Academy… "For a job thing."

She already didn't like lying to Neil, but she had to hope that what he didn't know wouldn't hurt him. They'd go their separate ways, and he'd never know any different. When they reached their destination, she would start putting the plan into motion.

Right. Her plan. It wasn't a good one. She liked to have weeks to work out every little detail. To figure out everything that could go wrong. To make up several escape plans just in case one failed. If this all went wrong, which was very likely, it could end one of three ways. She would be captured and thrown into some dark hole where she would spend the remainder of her days. Or she would be captured but could find a way to escape. That was easier said than done. A small fox, even one with the ability to camouflage herself, against a whole campus filled with shifters being trained to save the world wasn't good odds. She'd end up being torn to shreds.

And lastly? She completed the job, got back home, and was promptly betrayed by the Broker. There was no way she could see herself walking away from this scot-free. Why *wouldn't* this mysterious person betray her? If he'd found out who she was and realized he could so easily pull her strings, then he'd do it again and again and again…

She sighed.

One thing all three scenarios had in common? Neil wasn't in them. There was no way he could be. She was going to betray him. It didn't matter how he made her feel. It also didn't matter how much her fox liked him. It didn't even matter if it was the best sex she had ever had.

Neil wasn't her endgame. He was a means to an end.

LIZZIE WAS BACK IN HER JEANS AND T-SHIRT BY THE TIME Neil woke up. She'd been just about to try to deal with her hair, which had dried in a wild mess of curls while she'd slept, when she had a sudden flashback to when she was a kid, running around the garden with Amanda. She rubbed the palm of her hand against her forehead.

"Are you okay?" Neil asked.

"I'm fine." She looked up to see Neil's reflection in the dresser mirror. He looked like a man well satisfied with himself, not smug, but happy and tired. For a moment, the image filled her with happiness, but she had to push it away. This wasn't something to get used to. It also wasn't something she'd ever experienced before. She always made sure that her past partners never outstayed their welcome. She went to their place and was gone by the morning. It was simpler than that.

"I made coffee," she quickly added, gesturing to the cup she'd left for him on the bedside table. "When were you thinking of leaving?"

He blinked a few times. Then he picked up the coffee and breathed in the scent. "In a couple of hours. I don't know about you, but I worked up quite the appetite last night. There's a nice pancake place around the corner, if you're interested."

"I could eat, yeah."

"Then let's get some breakfast." He pushed the sheets off and strolled to the bathroom like he didn't have a care in the world.

A smile crept across her face like she didn't have any control over it. Then she shook her head. She knew what she needed to do. Last night she had given in to her desires, but she couldn't lose her senses about it. She had to keep her head in the game. It was wishful thinking on her part to think this could be a normal relationship scenario.

Her sister's life was at stake.

AFTER THEY FINISHED BREAKFAST THEY HAD TO GO PICK UP Neil's car from airport parking. They'd been in such a rush to get to the hotel last night that they didn't bother with it.

He popped the boot and put their bags inside. Though she was more than capable of looking after her bags, she didn't bother protesting. She liked how self-assured he was.

Besides, a huge yawn overtook her.

"Tired?" Neil asked.

"A little." When was the last time she'd had a complete

body workout? If she weren't a shifter with a remarkable healing ability, she would have been sore for a couple of days. Her other partners had been human, and she hadn't experienced anything as physical as sex with a shifter before.

He closed the trunk and stepped over to her, pulling her close. She gasped in surprise as he kissed her. It was a soft kiss, almost sweet, and as her hand reached up to caress his cheek, he broke their kiss and pressed his forehead against hers.

"I don't know what happens between us now, but I wanted to kiss you."

Her whole face burned, and there was no way he could miss the effect one simple kiss had on her. She quickly pulled away from him and headed to the passenger's seat.

"I should have said it earlier but what happened was a one-time thing," she said when he settled into the driver's seat. Though the words hurt her like a stab to the gut, they had to be said. She'd tried to say it in the restaurant, but she hadn't been able to push the words out. Now was the time.

"What?"

"I'm not interested in continuing whatever this is for the long term." She hated saying those words, too. How was it possible he'd gotten under her skin in such a short amount of time?

"Oh, okay." He started the car and backed out of the parking spot.

Didn't he want to talk about it? Or was he giving her space? Maybe he didn't believe her... The thoughts raced through her head. Her fox howled in frustration.

Finally, he answered her questions. "Have you forgotten we can detect lies? Sweetheart, my wolf knows your heart is racing a mile a minute, and I sensed the way your body reacted to my kiss just a moment ago."

"A gentleman wouldn't mention it."

"A gentleman wouldn't have slept with you last night," he countered, his words like a caress against her skin. "He wouldn't have held your hair in his fist and pleasured your body in every way that made you scream."

There was a long pause while they pulled up to the cashier and he paid for his parking. When he turned onto the highway, he spoke again. "If you don't want to continue this, that's fine. My offer of driving you to the Academy wasn't tied to you sleeping with me. Just be honest with yourself. You want me as much as I want you."

***

THEY STOPPED A FEW TIMES FOR FOOD, BUT THEY DIDN'T talk. Lizzie took the time to enjoy her new surroundings. She'd never been to Canada before. She'd spent most of her life in or around London, an urban jungle and a world away from the lush green fields and mountains. It was beautiful, and her fox was desperate to experience her new surroundings.

"When was the last time you shifted?"

It was the first thing he had said to her in hours. "Couple of days ago, why?"

"It's been longer for me. I'm going to want to shift tonight. Are you okay with that?"

She frowned. Sure, she wanted to explore, take in the new scents, but it was a bad idea. Her fox was desperate to come out and meet Neil's wolf, but that kind of intimacy would be just as bad as sleeping with him again.

"Do whatever you want." She tried to sound nonchalant, but if his lie-detector antenna was up, he'd easily identify the spark of excitement coursing through her at the thought of seeing his animal.

"I'll find somewhere after dinner."

CHAPTER SIX

WHILE HE SUSSED OUT THE FACT THAT LIZZIE WAS LYING about not wanting him anymore, he couldn't discern the reason why. Was she ashamed of sleeping with a stranger?

He was pretty sure that it wasn't something he'd done wrong, because they had a great night together. When they weren't lost in each other's bodies, they had talked, getting to know each other.

Was that it? Had they shared too much? Was she now feeling too intimate and vulnerable?

His wolf still chanted the word *mate*, a constant whisper in the back of his head. She shouldn't feel exposed with him. She should feel protected. Cherished, adored.

That was if this thought his wolf was having was correct. Neil didn't have any firsthand experience with the mating call. The only people he knew who'd experienced it were Jackson and Aubrey. At least, from what he understood about their whirlwind romance, they had both figured it out and accepted they were mates.

He was in a constant state of hyperawareness in Lizzie's presence. The way she moved, tucked her hair behind her ears, nibbled on her bottom lip. There wasn't anything about her that didn't call to him. She would need to accept it; you couldn't deny a mating call without some serious repercussions.

Was he ready to face the truth?

Not necessarily. At least not before he knew whether or not it was possible for one shifter to feel a mating pull toward someone who didn't also feel it. Lizzie hadn't shown she felt anything but a cordial kindness and then also some lust for him. Nothing to indicate her fox was also screaming *mate*. If she were feeling it, wouldn't she have mentioned it?

Why would she? You haven't to her, his wolf reminded him.

The goddess had a twisted sense of humor. Neil had laughed at the thought of Jackson and Aubrey ending up together, the lion and the mouse. Now his destined mate lived halfway across the world and he happened to meet her on an international flight.

He continued to drive for another couple of hours, and soon there were no other cars on the road going either way. They'd driven for so long that the songs on the radio had started to repeat. Then the upbeat tracks gave way to the hour of love. He could have laughed. Lizzie had tried dismissing anything romantic between them, and now for the next sixty minutes, they were going to be listening to nothing but love songs.

Not necessarily. There was a way to escape it. He pulled the car down a small dirt road and drove for a while before pulling over by some trees. Lizzie had been dozing, but he caught the precise moment when she realized they were stopping.

"Are you going to shift *now*?" she asked as he opened the door. "I thought you'd wait until we got to the hotel or something."

He walked round to her side of the car but didn't answer her. Instead, he opened the back door and started taking his clothes off. He tossed his boots into the car, unbuttoned his jeans, and pulled his T-shirt over his head, happy to let Lizzie look if she wanted to. He kept himself in decent shape, which was easier for a shifter than a regular human. He only stepped into a gym when he needed to blow off some steam, yet his muscles stayed ripped.

He saw Lizzie watching him out of the corner of his eye, but when he turned his head toward her, she quickly faced forward. He smiled as he pushed down his jeans and boxers, and both went onto the backseat with everything else. He had no problem with being naked in front of her. He hadn't been lying when he said he hadn't shifted in a while, but he also liked how she looked at him like he was a thick steak she wanted to take a bite out of.

"Do you want to join me?"

"No." Her voice was high-pitched.

"Fine. I'll be back in about half an hour. Try not to get into trouble."

He stepped forward, and the change swept over him. There was a fine line between pleasure and pain. Being his wolf was an intricate part of him but more like a limb that had fallen asleep. Pins and needles erupted over him as his body transformed. His nose stretched and morphed into a snout. Fur covered his entire body, and his hands and feet became paws. He landed with four legs on the ground and looked over his shoulder in Lizzie's direction.

In this form, his baser instincts were close to the surface.

Bite. Claim. Mate.

I agree with you. She is ours, but we can't take the choice away from her. She isn't ready. She's scared.

It took every ounce of mental strength to move away from her.

We wouldn't hurt her.

I know.

Lizzie watched him, her lids heavy and lips parted. She was fighting against her need for him, that much was clear, but it was a problem for another day. He ran into the field behind him.

Now, he was more certain than he'd been before. Being in his wolf form gave him a closer connection to his senses, and it was clear as day: he and Lizzie were destined to be together.

He just had to wait for her to come around to the idea.

The wind pushed the fur away from his face as he sprinted. It was good to stretch his legs. To let his brain forget every human worry, every issue he had to deal with at work, and just *be free.*

Neil was trained to be a highly effective agent, excellent at gathering information. He could kill a man with a well-placed spoon, but he spent most of his time behind a computer. He preferred it that way. He liked working behind the scenes, keeping Jackson safe.

But he loved to let his wolf out and run just as much as the next shifter did.

As the sun began to set, he turned in the field, running back toward the car, but he stopped short when he saw movement in the long grass in front of him. He crouched, lowering his belly close to the ground. He listened and sniffed.

He recognized the scent, even though it held a note of something different and unfamiliar.

Lizzie.

He didn't move. Why had she followed him into the field after saying she wasn't going to? There was more movement in front of him, and he crept forward. Where was she? He sniffed, hoping her scent would narrow down her location. Nothing.

Then, something landed on him. He rolled onto his back, and the creature jumped off him before he could capture her.

But she stayed within eyesight, and he took in the view of the beautiful white creature who watched him with a playful expression in her auburn eyes. She wasn't like other foxes he'd seen. Her ears were large and her body small and compact. Her fluffy tail moved slowly behind her while she continued to stare at him. Goddess, she was beautiful.

She darted off into the thick crops, and Neil gave chase. For someone who had been moving around making all sorts of commotion a moment ago, she was now silent. He could play the game the same way.

He laid on the ground and rested his snout on top of his paws. He was trained to hunt, be patient, and strike at the right moment. She would slip up. A twig broke some-where to his left, but he didn't pounce. Instead, he dashed to the right and caught sight of her bushy tail. Using his powerful back legs, he leaped, coming down above her and grabbing her with his paws, careful not to hurt her.

When they rolled to a stop, he nipped the back of her neck. His message was clear, even for someone who hadn't grown up with shifters. He was telling her that he won, which meant she needed to surrender, to submit to him.

She made a high-pitched noise, and for a second, he thought he had hurt her, but then she turned around and licked his nose.

The sun had set, and the sky was now dark but full of stars. The change back to his human form was much easier, and Lizzie followed him. They lay naked next to each other, her head on his chest. Neil loved it here. Sure, he knew how important his job was, and he was very good at what he did, but sometimes he preferred the quiet of the outdoors.

"Why did you change your mind?"

"I've never shifted with another shifter. It was an opportunity I didn't want to miss."

For a split second, he could taste the bitter aftertaste of a lie. Not that she'd never run with another shifter. He believed Lizzie when she said she didn't have experience with other shifters. The lie was that she'd shifted for the general experience, when the truth was she wanted to be with *him*. It was personal. He wasn't just any old shifter she could have an experience with. He was her mate.

And she knew it.

But he'd let it slide.

It would have been easy to question her, to get her to admit her feelings toward him, but it wouldn't accomplish anything. As long as she wasn't ready for the truth, she would keep trying to push him away. Denying the truth. The last thing he wanted to do was make her run.

He might have accepted the beautiful fox in his arms was his mate, but Lizzie still needed time to grapple with the idea herself.

She rolled onto his chest, and he readjusted her in his arms. She glanced up, resting her chin on top of her hands. Wild white curls circled her face, her cupid bow-shaped lips, and those amber eyes. His heart ached in a way he didn't think was even possible.

"What are you thinking?"

"How stunning you are. How beautiful this moment is. How I could stay here forever with you in my arms."

She didn't break eye contact with him, but he caught the moment her cheeks reddened. "You've got a way with words. I hope whatever company you work for knows how good you are."

Then, she kissed him. It was a soft kiss, peppered with nibbles along his bottom lip. They were surrounded by tall crops and the long road was deserted, so he felt free to pull her into a tight hug, crushing her breasts against his chest. He slipped his tongue inside her warm mouth.

He rolled them until she was on her back, looking up at him. No one looked at him the way she did. Did she even know what she was doing?

The night before in the hotel had been frantic. His need for her had been intense in a way he had never experienced before. Now, he wanted to take his time with her. To worship her body.

He found the sweet spot underneath her ear, nibbling, kissing, and blowing against the now damp spot. She wriggled against him and tried to pull her hands free.

She moaned. "I want to touch you."

"I'm not finished," he whispered against her ear. "You need to beg before I give you what you need."

"Oh really?" She laughed.

"Yeah." He rolled his hips, letting her feel every inch of him against her thigh. "Put your hands above your head."

She didn't argue with him but did what he had asked.

"Good girl."

He turned his attention to her breasts, flicking and teasing each nipple until they were rock hard. Her moaning grew louder, and as he reached a hand between her thighs, her hips bucked. She was slick underneath his questing fingertips. With soft strokes he continued to touch her, stopping short of pushing inside of her.

Her body glistened with sweat, her breathing heavy. It wouldn't take much to push her over the edge. He removed his hand, and Lizzie flinched.

"What are you doing?"

"Getting into a better position."

He moved down, crawling lower until his face was between her legs and his lips right at her sex. He guided her feet to his shoulders, opening her up to him. "The rule is the same. If you move or try and touch me, I'll stop and we'll both go back to the car unsatisfied."

He started nibbling on the top of her thighs, ignoring the sweet heat between her legs. She started moving her hips, a gentle rise and fall that could have been an unconscious movement. He wouldn't punish her for that.

"Neil…"

"What?"

"Neil…" Her whole body arched.

"Tell me what you want, sweetheart, and I'll give it to you."

"Taste me," she moaned. "Please I need you."

That was all he needed to hear. With his arms around her thighs and his hands on her hips, holding her in place, he breathed in her sweet scent and gave her what she wanted.

CHAPTER SEVEN

There was something different about this. Their time in the hotel had been a rush to release tension. The need to get him out of his clothes and inside of her overrode every ounce of common sense she possessed. She'd reasoned that it had been a one-time thing and, once the pent-up lust was released, she'd be able to resist future encounters.

Lizzie had made herself a promise that she would try and at least keep a distance between them. That she wouldn't give in to the blinding need she had for him. He was a stranger, but why couldn't she ignore the way he called her?

Was her reaction to him something to do with being a shifter?

She didn't have time to ponder the question. A spike of pleasure hit her, and she cried out. In the middle of nowhere, with a blanket of stars above them, they could have been the only two people on the planet. It was perfect. She pushed all her doubts to the back of her mind. Every flick of his tongue chased the impending threat of what she had to do to a dark corner of her mind. She would worry about it tomorrow. Nothing was going to change what she needed to do to keep her sister safe.

Amanda didn't know the danger she was in. It was up to Lizzie to protect her. But right now, she couldn't do anything about it, so why not enjoy the moment with Neil?

Another bolt of pleasure hit her. The urge to touch him was overwhelming, but she was a willing participant in his game, and he'd threatened to stop if she touched him. That was the last thing she wanted.

The orgasm hit her with a speed and intensity that made her head throb in pain. Another one followed, and she bit her bottom lip. She didn't think she could take any more. Even the slightest brush of crisp cool air against her sensitive lips was too much.

Neil worked his way back up her body, trailing kisses along her hip bone and the dip of her stomach, stopping at her breasts. She continued to watch him. Even if her eyelids were heavy, she could still peek out from underneath her lashes. The way he used the flat of his tongue to tease her nipples into hard peaks felt amazing. He nibbled them, and every bite sent another bolt to her core.

"Neil…" She didn't even know what to say.

"Are you enjoying this?"

"You know I am," she managed to say as he teased her tender folds. "I want to feel you inside of me."

"You want or need?"

"I need." As soon as the words left her lips, he slipped a finger inside of her, stretching her. Her fox basked in the attention he gave her. *Ours.* "Fuck."

"Soon, sweetheart." Her whole body was hot as he continued to work her body. "I think you can give me one more. Have a look."

She didn't even realize she'd closed her eyes. The first thing she saw was Neil's dark eyes. In that moment, he looked wolfish, like the animal he could shift into. Half draped over her, she had a clear line of sight of his hand, his fingers pushing inside of her. It looked incredibly hot. The orgasm that hit her was harder, and as the scream ripped through her, Neil put a hand over her mouth, muffling the sound.

She was still sensitive as he got into position above her, picking up her legs and resting her feet over his shoulders. His gaze never left hers as he thrust inside of her in one smooth motion. Her mind fractured like a kaleidoscope as he chased his release. A groan escaped his lips.

"Oh fuck, Lizzie. I love you."

Did he really just say that? She should panic. Run. *Something.*

But both her fox side and her human side felt nothing but content.

SOMETHING TICKLED AGAINST THE SIDE OF HIS FACE. NEIL brushed his face and then opened his eyes. They were still in the field. The morning sun cast everything in a warm orange glow. Lizzie was curled up by his side, fast asleep. He took the opportunity to study her face. She looked younger, somehow more innocent. Even if he knew she wasn't. The things they had done together would have made a lesser man blush. Neil, on the other hand, had found peace. Jackson had said finding Aubrey was like finding the other half of the puzzle. Neil hadn't understood that until now.

He brushed a strand of hair away from her face then trailed a path down her cheek to her lips. Then he froze as a memory hit him. *I love you.* Holy fuck, had he said that while they were having sex? Being careful not to wake her, he collapsed onto the ground.

Everyone knew that you never made a huge declaration of love during the heat of the moment. It was a cliche, like something in a bad romance book. They hadn't even talked about the future. She didn't even know about the mating bond. She was going to think he was insane. That he'd been caught up in a fling that was destined to end. He hadn't even told her the truth about who he was.

"Well done, Yun. You're fucking this up."

She shuffled next to him, and he glanced down. The expression in her amber eyes was cautious, and she sat up. "You make a habit of talking to yourself?"

"Not as a general rule."

Should he bring it up now? He shook his head. Shifters were more than comfortable with a little bit of nakedness, but serious conversations required clothes. He couldn't let there be any misunderstanding; she had to know how he felt about her. The mating bond was hard to explain to a human, and with her lack of experience with the shifter world, he imagined it was going to be a hard sell.

"Let's get some clothes on before the car gets reported as abandoned." He stood and offered his hand to her.

She glanced at his hand, and for a second, he didn't think she'd take the offer of help. Then she slipped her small hand into his, and he pulled her up. "Do you think that'll happen?"

"It's possible. Let's not risk it."

They got back to the car, and in the awkward silence, they got dressed. There was no way she hadn't heard those three words when he'd uttered them.

He watched as she opened the trunk and retrieved a bottle of water. She tipped some of the clean liquid into her hand and flicked it onto her face.

"Are you okay?" he asked.

"I need a shower."

"Starting to feel a little grimy?"

"A little. I don't mind traveling, but I prefer when I'm staying in a hotel with hot water."

"I'm staying at Jackson's, but I don't think he'll mind you making use of their shower before you head to the Academy."

"I was hoping to get a room in a motel." The water bottle slipped out of her hand, and she swore.

She bent down and picked it up.

Neil opened the driver's side door but stopped short of getting inside when she said, "I mean I'm sure your friends are great, but I don't want to inconvenience them."

"You wouldn't be, but that's okay." He stopped himself from adding that he could always stay with her.

He'd find the time within the next couple of hours to broach the mate topic with her. He didn't know how she would handle it; some women liked the idea of hooking up with a FUC agent. The element of danger was a thrill, but Lizzie might not feel that way.

"Let's go."

CHAPTER EIGHT

Lizzie couldn't remember the last time she'd spent so much time with someone.

After their night in the field, she expected them to have an awkward start to the day, but it wasn't. They had gotten used to each other's company, and the car ride felt as natural as anything else.

She leaned out of the window and spread her hand out, twisting her hand in the wind. She knew Neil was watching her. Even with his gaze on the road, he was in a constant state of awareness when she was concerned. It might work out to be a problem later, but she would face it when she didn't have another choice.

It was dangerous to forget why she was traveling to the Academy. She was there to steal a rare book. The threat to her sister and the needle at her throat gave her the impression this was something that couldn't be picked up from any old bookshop.

"I'm sure Jackson and Aubrey would like to meet you."

It was a dangerous move to put herself on the radar of

an agent of the FUC. She hadn't been lying when she said to Neil that she hadn't had any real connection with other shifters, and she couldn't forget that she was there to *rob* FUCN'A. So far, she'd managed to stay off the FUC radar. Now, she was about to walk into the lion's den. The irony wasn't lost on her.

"This was just supposed to be casual, remember?" She spoke softly.

He squeezed her thigh, and heat shot went through her. "It's just that you said you haven't been around shifters much, and I thought visiting them might help you get ready for walking into FUCN'A and being surrounded by our kind."

"Uh, I think I'll be okay."

"Do you want to tell me what's on your mind?"

More than anything. When did this get so complicated? "There's nothing on my mind. Just thinking about the upcoming job thing."

"Oh. All right."

After a moment, she realized how rude she must have sounded. "I don't mean to offend your friend."

Neil tapped the steering wheel in time with the music. "He isn't just my friend. I didn't have anyone growing up. I was abandoned when I was a baby."

"You were?" She cocked her head to the side. This was another thing that connected them. "Do you know what happened to your parents?"

"They decided they didn't want a kid. Sometimes it's just as simple as that."

Her mother had died when Lizzie was born, and her dad put her into care. The Adamses adopted her when she was a baby. She knew she was lucky. She'd had a cooky old neighbor woman who'd kept an eye on her, and when she had started to shift, the woman let her in on the shifter secret and warned her against letting anyone know, even her adoptive family. It wouldn't have surprised her if Delia and Ernie Adams would have tried to get rid of a child who wasn't human.

"My bio-dad was like that."

"You ever try to track him down?"

She shook her head. "Ernie was my dad. He taught me how to ride a bike. He kept me safe. Whoever my dad was before him, it doesn't matter. So how did you meet Jackson?"

If she had been looking out of the window, she would have missed the way his knuckles turned white as his grip tightened on the steering wheel.

"Did you meet at school?"

"It's safe to say we grew up in different worlds. Have you ever heard of Holt Industries?"

The name did ring a bell. "Your best friend is Jackson Holt?" She had read about the wayward son of Cassandra Holt.

He chuckled. "Yeah. The misadventures of Jackson and Neil. His parents unofficially adopted me while I was in high school."

It was starting to feel like he was dancing around the subject. "How did you meet him?"

"In agent training."

For a second she couldn't process what he'd said. They'd trained together? To be agents? *FUC* agents? Neil was FUC?

Ohh, this was bad. Lizzie had fucked up. She'd been sleeping with a FUC agent, one who had ties to a place she was targeting for her next robbery. Lizzie took a deep breath and tried to school her face and heart rate into indifference. He couldn't know what those words did to her.

"You told me you were in communications."

"I am. Did you think I meant something like selling cable TV and internet packages?" There was no denying the tension in the shared space. He was worried about her impending reaction. His grip on the steering wheel had gotten worse. If he didn't loosen his grip, he was going to break it.

"You're an agent."

"Is that a problem?"

She wanted to scream *yes*. It *was* a problem. A big one. There was no way she was going to be able to sneak into the Academy without becoming prime suspect number one. All he had to do was ask that Alyce Cooper woman if she had asked a fennec fox shifter to come meet with her and he'd know that she'd been lying the whole time.

"I wish you'd told me," she said finally.

"Would it have made a difference?"

"Maybe... I don't know." The tension in the car was unbearable. Her fox paced inside of her. She didn't like how what happened between them was unraveling in front of her and there was nothing she could do to stop it. It was like she could sense Neil's wolf's panic. Her fingers ached. She wanted to reach out and touch him, comfort him. Instead, she clutched her hands into fists.

"Lizzie..."

She couldn't figure out what to say. If he knew why she was there, he would think she had targeted him. Sure, she had intended to use him, but finding him had been a stroke of good luck. It hadn't been nefarious.

"Why do I feel this way?" She hadn't meant to say anything. Her thoughts were a tangled mess. "Why can I sense your wolf?"

"You know why."

"I don't."

He hit his brakes and pulled the car over to the side of the road, parking and turning to face her. Lizzie held herself still. If he touched her now, she would be lost.

They sat in silence. Lizzie didn't even know where they were. They had another couple of hours of travel before they reached the Academy, but she had put her trust in Neil. Her first mistake.

"You know why," he said again. "You didn't grow up with shifters, but that doesn't matter. That call you feel inside of you? The urge to touch me, to be near me when I'm off in the field or whatever? The hum of energy between us... The ache." He reached out, and she moved away from him, but there was nowhere to hide in the car. "Both parts of you like me. Are drawn to me."

Was it as simple as that? Lizzie knew her fox liked him. That was one of the reasons she found herself getting out of the car last night and following him. Even when she'd told him that she wouldn't. "I've never been with a shifter. Isn't this how it is with any one of them?"

"No, not with any one of them. Just certain ones. The best way to describe it is every emotion is heightened. I know this is complicated." His voice was husky, and their gazes locked. There it was again. It felt like an invisible cord snapped into place between them.

She licked her bottom lip. All she wanted to do was kiss him. As if her body had a life of its own, she edged closer to him. He unclipped her seat belt, and she sat on his lap. The strength in his arms amazed her. The way he controlled her body, moving her into the exact position he wanted her.

"I'm angry with you," she grumbled.

"I know." He brushed a kiss against her lips, and she opened for him.

"I'm still leaving after my business at the Academy. This isn't some Hallmark movie where I give up my life and stay here." She moaned as he turned his attention to a spot on her neck that chased all reasonable thoughts away. The roads were deserted, but they wouldn't stay that way for long.

"We'll figure it out." He gripped her hips, moving her against him in a maddening rhythm. She gasped as his rock-hard erection brushed against her.

No, we won't. "It's not going to work."

"We don't know that." He pushed his hands up the back of her shirt and held her close. "I don't want to give this up."

"I don't like people keeping secrets from me," she mumbled against his neck. He didn't have to know she kept a pretty big secret from him. "Is there anything else you want to tell me?"

He paused. "You might want to get off me."

The atmosphere in the car had changed. Lizzie got off him and sat back in her seat. She pulled her legs up to her chest. What else could he tell her? His being an agent was a big secret and something she wouldn't be able to ignore. When they had first met, Lizzie had made the decision that her sister was more important. She would betray him in a heartbeat and wouldn't even blink. That had changed. She now knew she would hesitate. She didn't want to hurt him.

"Neil?"

He turned the car on and merged back onto the main road. "How much do you know about the shifter world?"

"Not much." He didn't know that was by choice. "I know about the Academy and the agents. That's about it."

"You haven't heard about the mating bond?" He glanced at her before turning his attention back to the road.

She shook her head as her fox howled *Ours*. She frowned. "A part of me knows the term. What does it mean?"

"It's a little like soulmates. That's a human term. You've heard of that one?"

She nodded.

"It's a phenomenon, two or more people destined to be together forever. It's fate."

She bristled at the word. She wanted to argue with him. She didn't believe in fate; her life was planned out with such care that every eventuality was accounted for. Everything but him. "You're saying this is something out of our control? That's it's predetermined? I don't believe in that."

"You might not, but it doesn't make it any less true. You're my mate."

"Don't you think you're reading into it a little too much? I mean you already confessed to loving me." She smiled to take the harshness out of her words. "It's a little dramatic to say we're destined to be together."

"Don't you feel it too?"

"I don't know what I feel," she admitted. "I don't know how many times I have to say this, but I'm not staying here, Neil. My life is in the UK. This doesn't change anything."

"I'm not asking you to stay. I know this is a lot to take in, but I think we can find a way to make this work. Can you at least think about it?"

There was nothing to think about. They had a time limit. By the end of the week, she needed to be back home, *if* she managed to get out of FUC with the book.

Neil wasn't in her future. She didn't even know if she had a future.

"I'll think about it."

She lied.

CHAPTER NINE

The scenery was beautiful with the mountains on the horizon and the smaller towns he drove through, but it wasn't *that* interesting.

She was putting distance between them.

When Neil couldn't take the silence anymore, he put the radio on. He had given her a lot to process in a short amount of time. He never thought he would have to explain the mating bond to his own mate. Lizzie hadn't even looked at him when she told him she would think about the future of their relationship.

He should have told her earlier. It didn't matter over-all, because even if she wasn't ready to accept what he had told her, it didn't make it any less true. The goddess had brought her into his life now, and there had to be a reason for that.

The sun had started to set again as they drove into Nowheresville. He went past Aubrey's house, where a light was on in the living room, and continued to the one lone bed and breakfast, opting for that over the local hotel, which was usually full of one biker group or another.

He didn't know the precise moment Lizzie had fallen asleep, but she was snoring when he pulled into the parking lot.

"Lizzie?"

She blinked a few times and sat up. "Are we here?"

"Just pulled in. Are you sure that you want to stay here?"

"Yes."

"Do you want me to come and collect you in the morning and take you up to the Academy?"

For a second she looked conflicted, but then she nodded and got out of the car.

Had she planned on inviting him in with her? Neil followed her. He could at least walk her to the door.

It was a beautiful night, and he liked being away from normal civilization. All of that was forgotten as his wolf paced restlessly inside of him. He didn't want to leave her side. It didn't matter that Nowheresville was the safest place on the planet. Not counting the problems they had half a year ago, nothing exciting happened. Lizzie went to the trunk and found the button to open it then pulled out her bag. Neil closed the trunk, and Lizzie turned to face him.

He didn't give her a chance to speak. He cupped her face and drew her closer. There wasn't much chance of keeping the kiss sweet and chaste. As soon as their mouths brushed against each other, the need to deepen overwhelmed him. But this had to stop happening. He needed to give her alone time to think and process every-thing that was happening between them.

He stepped away. "I'll see you in the morning."

She nodded and turned away, heading for the building. He returned to his car and waited for her to go up the steps and inside.

She didn't even look back at him.

His wolf howled mournfully. It took every ounce of will for Neil not to turn the car off, stalk into the bed and break-fast, throw her over his shoulder, and take her with him.

No, he couldn't do that. She had made it clear that she didn't want to go with him, and he needed to respect that. When he reached Aubrey and Jackson's place again, he parked in the driveway and gathered his belongings. He closed the trunk, and the front door opened. His best friend dashed down the steps and pulled him into a hug, lifting him clear off his feet.

Jackson Holt was a big man and wouldn't have been out of place as one of those mythical warriors from Ancient Greece. His mane of blond hair had a permanent wave to it and reached his shoulders. That style on any other man would have been feminine, but Jackson had never been described that way.

When he finished trying to crack Neil's spine, he put him down. "We thought you would get here yesterday. Are you hungry? Aubrey just finished cooking."

"I could eat a horse."

Jackson patted him on the back as they walked back to the house. "What took you so long?"

"I found my mate."

His best friend closed the door behind them. The majority of Aubrey's house was an open plan, and Neil spied the mouse shifter in the kitchen, her dark brunette hair tied up into a messy bun. She gave him a half wave before she turned her attention back to her task. Aubrey didn't own a television, and much of her wall space in the living room was filled with bookcases. There were hints that Jackson lived there as well. A couple of pairs of boots by the front door and photos on the wall.

"You found your mate." Jackson repeated the words and cast a glance at Aubrey before turning back to Neil. "And she's where, exactly?"

Jackson made to turn around, to look back outside, but Neil stopped him. "She's staying at the B&B."

"She could have stayed here."

"I know. It's complicated."

Aubrey appeared from the kitchen carrying a tray, which she practically vanished behind. Jackson rushed forward to take it from her. "You should have told me it was finished. I would have helped."

She smacked his arm and smiled. "I'm not an invalid."

"Let me decide how to take care of my mate, woman." He put everything on the table and turned to face Neil, the look on his face filled with expectation.

That was when Neil noticed Aubrey's bump. He blinked a few times in surprise before he hugged her. "That's new. Why didn't you tell me over the phone?"

She touched her stomach. "We didn't want to ruin the surprise. Come on. Let's sit, and you can tell us why your relationship with your mate is complicated."

"We don't have to talk about that."

"I'll go grab the beer," Jackson called out as he walked back into the kitchen.

"AND THAT'S WHAT HAPPENED."

Neil hadn't thought it was a long story, but by the time he had finished telling it, the three of them had gone through a couple of stacks of barbecue ribs. Aubrey was glowing, and for such a small person, she put away a lot of food. Neil was on his second beer, and he noticed that Jackson hadn't touched his. Thanks to a high metabolism, shifters had a hard time getting drunk, but that didn't mean Neil didn't feel like trying.

"Are you sure she's your mate?" Aubrey asked as she wiped her lips with a cloth.

"Never been surer of anything. She grew up with humans, and while she knew she was a shifter, she doesn't have much experience with our world. She's fighting against the idea."

"I can't blame her for that. It's a lot to take on faith." She leaned back in her chair, her hand resting on top of her stomach. "The idea of predetermined mates is a hard pill to swallow."

"How long is she staying in town?" Jackson asked as he picked up a burger. There was a lot of food for three people. Aubrey must have been cooking for hours.

"A couple of days."

"And what do you want from her?" Aubrey prodded. "You need a plan. You're a FUC agent; you travel all over the world. You've said yourself your lifestyle isn't one conducive for relationships. You're asking a lot from her if you expect her to stay."

"I don't want her to feel trapped," Neil assured her. "This isn't some ploy to keep her, but we all know what happens when you refuse the mating bond. That need doesn't go away just because you don't want it. We would have to find a way of making it work. You two did."

Aubrey and Jackson exchanged a fond smile.

"It was easier for us. Aubrey's work with the Bathory book is important to the FUC, so having me here as a bodyguard helps. The Broker hasn't tried anything else." The last words were more of a rumble in his chest. The memory of nearly losing his mate wasn't something he enjoyed reliving. "Thank goddess we're at the end of it though. She has to wrap it up at the end of this week, when FUC is taking it to some hidden secure location."

"And what happens then? You'll go back to work?"

"I signed my transfer." Jackson winced as he said it.

"Transfer? To what office?" Neil wracked his brain for where Jackson might want to move to. And why hadn't he spoken to Neil about it before signing the papers? They were a team, and Neil would need to transfer as well.

"No office." Jackson adjusted himself in his chair, clearly uncomfortable. "I'm going to be moving here and transferring to the Academy to work as a teacher, training new cadets."

Of course he was. Neil wasn't surprised, but he was also caught unaware. What was the rush? He'd figured they'd still be able to get a few more good years as agents in before Jackson made the change.

Neil looked down at Aubrey's stomach again. Of

course. Jackson lost his father at a young age, and there was no way he wanted to miss a moment of his kid's life.

Aubrey interrupted the silence by standing up, her hand on her lower back. "I think this child has decided to use my bladder as a soccer ball. But don't mind me. You two should go for a run."

Jackson stood, towering over his mate and needing to bend down to brush a kiss against the top of her head. "Don't worry about making up his bed. I'll do it."

"I'm a grown-ass man. I can sort out my bed," Neil grumbled. "You're not even parents yet. You don't get to practice your skills on me."

His best friend slung his arm over his shoulder and directed him to the back door. The last time he'd been there, there had been a pretty garden with hanging plants behind the house and a winding path down to a gate. On the other side was a field of tall grass. Neil flashed back to the night before, and a tightness settled in the pit of his stomach. It had gone bad so quickly that he hadn't even had time to process what had happened. Lizzie was pulling away from him, and his wolf had become a moody teenager overnight.

Neil sat down and took a long pull on his lukewarm beer. Jackson sat opposite him. Jackson's motorcycle was parked in the back garden, a sheet over it to protect it from the worse of the weather.

"What's up, Jackson?"

The lion shifter reached into the inside pocket of his jacket and pulled out some papers with a pen. Neil frowned as he took the offered papers and started to read.

For a second he couldn't process what he was seeing. "Is this what I think it is?"

Jackson smiled. "Yeah."

'You want me to be the godfather to your child?" It wasn't even a question. He was just stunned at the request.

"I've always thought of us as family."

Neil frowned. "You have a mother, who might kill me when she finds out you want me to look after her grandchild."

"This is a worst-case scenario. Aubrey and I would like to live till we're old and grey, but we wanted to tick this one off. What do you say?"

Neil looked at the paper and all the legal terms he couldn't even begin to understand. Then he glanced back up at his friend, the closest thing he had to family. "I'd be honored.

CHAPTER TEN

THE FIRST THING LIZZIE DID WAS COLLAPSE ONTO THE BED and close her eyes. What she wanted to do was get into the shower, but the siren's call from the bed was harder to ignore. She ignored the pang of loneliness at being without him. Her fox was miserable. Her feelings echoed Lizzie's own. She did her best to ignore how sad she felt.

It was stupid.

She didn't know him.

Mate. Ours. There it was again. The soft voice in the back of her head was back. "I don't believe in that sort of thing."

Doesn't matter. Ours. Lizzie growled in frustration. She had things to do. Wallowing in self-pity wasn't even on the list she had in her head. She rolled off the bed and stepped into the bathroom. After a quick shower, she started to feel close to normal again.

She wrapped the bathrobe around her and tied a knot in the belt. Then she peered out of the window. She could see the road and the few nearby buildings but nothing else. They were in the middle of the woods and the mountains, but somewhere out there, the Academy was waiting. The *book* was waiting.

She needed to sneak into a place she had never been, find a book she didn't know where it was being kept in an unknown location, and make sure nobody figured out the truth about why she was there. It all sounded quite simple in her head, but she was wise enough to know better. It wasn't anywhere near easy. It wasn't even close. For whatever reason, the Broker was desperate, and he'd decided to use her for his urgent task.

She wanted to get in and out as quickly as possible. In an ideal world, she would sneak in tonight, grab the book, and be on the next plane out. There weren't any planes out though. Well, technically the Academy had one small hangar for their private planes, but that was far too obvious. Someone would notice a plane leaving on an unscheduled flight with an unknown pilot. That was a ballsy move and one she wouldn't be taking.

Stealing a car would be easier. She'd need to abandon it on the highway and use the burner phone to get an extraction. The Broker had been kind enough to leave her a contact number, one she had hoped not to use, but her options were drying up fast.

Neil had offered to drive her up to the Academy the next day. She wondered if she should ask him for a guided tour. It would give her a chance to walk around unnoticed, escorted by a FUC agent, who presumably would be authorized personnel there.

That would be the easiest way into the building. Then she would have plenty of time to do some scouting and figure out the placement of the cameras before she broke in during the night.

No. The least amount of time she had to spend with the man who called her his mate, the better.

I could always use the opportunity to say goodbye.

She got the distinct impression Neil didn't want to say goodbye. He would try and talk her into staying or figuring out a future together. A future she couldn't give him.

He'll help us.

Lizzie shook her head. She hated arguing with herself. It always resulted in a headache. It wasn't as simple as that. They were like two sides of a coin, the good and the bad, but they couldn't see each other. There wasn't any way they would work.

One more day. They would have one last day together, and then, by the weekend, Lizzie would be gone. Either to certain death or a life on the run. Amanda would be safe, and Lizzie would be able to go into hiding, at least for a little while, until the Broker found someone new to use as their puppet.

Lizzie crawled into bed and switched off the bedside lamp. London was a busy city. There was always some kind of noise—drunks, ambulances, and police sirens. In Nowheresville, there wasn't anything like that. Surprisingly, she had gotten used to the sounds of nature, and her fox had liked that a lot.

Unfortunately, she'd also gotten used to the feeling of Neil beside her, holding her close. Christ, she did miss him.

She grabbed a spare pillow and hugged it. It wasn't the

same, but Lizzie had to get used to the idea that she wouldn't be sleeping next to Neil ever again.

LIZZIE BLAMED OVERSLEEPING ON THE CRAZY LAST COUPLE of days she had.

On average she got five hours of sleep, six tops. When she looked at her watch, she frowned. *Eleven?*

She sat bolt upright in bed, awake and panicky. What on earth was wrong with her? Everything she had done over the last couple of days had been out of character. Neil had thrown her off balance.

She scrambled to get out of bed, and she rooted through her bag to find some clean clothes. How long did she have until Neil knocked on the door?

Not long it seemed, as someone knocked just then. Lizzie froze, but the scent wasn't Neil's. Nor was it the owner, Ms. "Please call me Martina, everyone does."

"Hello?" a strange woman's voice called out. "I was told you were still here."

Another knock.

Lizzie frowned. "Who's there?"

"My name is Aubrey. I'm friends with Neil."

Lizzie let out a breath and stalked toward the door. She unlocked and opened it to reveal a woman about the same height as herself. She had mousy brown hair and dark eyes. She was also very pregnant.

"Hello?" Lizzie was only half dressed, but she didn't want to turn her back on the stranger. Even a pregnant one.

"I'm sorry. I didn't know you were still getting dressed." She turned around, and Lizzie pulled on her clothes. The shower last night had left her white hair in disarray, but she couldn't do anything about it right now. When she was ready, she picked up her small black bag and slipped it into her pocket. It looked a little bulky, but the heavy leather of her jacket hid it well.

"Why are you here?" She didn't bother to hide the suspicious edge to her voice. She'd been mentally prepared for Neil, not the very pregnant woman.

"Neil is helping Jackson with something."

"So, he sent you?"

"I volunteered. He said you needed a ride to the Academy, and I said I can do it since I need to go to work." The woman pressed her lips together and then added, "He also thought you might want a little more space."

The gesture made Lizzie feel touched for a split second before she remembered she was trying to forget the man. She didn't want to be anywhere around him. The job was the most important thing. She had to keep her sister safe.

But then the name *Aubrey* rang a bell. The name Aubrey Taylor had been in the file the Broker had left her. She was the librarian who was working on the book. Was it possible the Aubrey that Neil had been talking about this whole time was the Aubrey she needed to look for?

"What do you do at the Academy?"

"I'm a librarian." The other woman leaned against the door frame, waiting for Lizzie to put her boots on. "I wanted to go in and collect some paperwork."

As much as Lizzie didn't believe in fate when it came

to mates, she wasn't going to look a gift horse in the mouth. This had to be Aubrey Taylor. The very one she was there to find.

She offered the mouse a smile, holding back from allowing it to look too predatory, lest she scare away the little mouse. "Thanks for offering to drive me." *And hopefully leading me straight to the FUCN'A library and the book that I need to steal.*

"You're from London?" Aubrey asked as they drove.

"Not really." Lizzie shrugged. "I was born and raised in a town a couple of hours north of the capital. Have you always lived in Nowheresville?"

Aubrey laughed. "I'm from a district near New York. Come from a small family, which is rare with mice. My parents were always a tad over-protective. The joys of being an only child I guess. Do you have any siblings?"

They hadn't been traveling for long, but Lizzie had already decided she liked Aubrey. A pang of guilt hit her when she realized the woman trusted her. A small part of Lizzie wanted to be indifferent to her. There was no reason she had to play nice to a woman she had met a few minutes ago, but there was something likable about the mouse shifter.

It was weird that Lizzie had spent a lifetime not creating emotional attachments, but being around Neil had opened the floodgates. It didn't matter how much she tried to keep a distance; she couldn't manage it anymore.

"A sister. But we're not close."

"Why aren't you close?"

"We just grew apart."

Aubrey must have sensed her discomfort because she didn't bring it up again. They drove through a gate, Aubrey using her staff pass to automatically open the gate.

Lizzie really had lucked out. She could have easily snuck onto the property in her fox form, but this was way easier.

Aubrey drove through the Academy grounds, and Lizzie looked around, watching in awe at all the shifter cadets doing exercises and training.

How many of them are mice like Aubrey, versus wolves like Neil or lions like Jackson?

While her research had told her the Academy took both predatory and prey, it was still the large predatory animals who had higher enrolment.

And who would have no problem taking out a fennec fox who didn't belong.

Aubrey parked her car in a space, and Lizzie got out of the car. The Academy was huge. The Broker had gotten a hold of some interesting information, things he'd been helpful enough to share with her in the files. There was a basement, a first floor, and a second. On the third floor were the dormitories. To the outside world, the old building housed the Animal Rescue Special House of Learning but appearances were deceiving.

The library was on the second floor. Lizzie thought that the book could be found there, but the Academy was a fortress. Nobody was stupid enough to try and break in. Nobody but her.

But she had a secret weapon. A trusting little mouse

who thought nothing of leading her mate's best friend's mate around.

Lizzie would be thankful for such small favors.

"How long have you worked here?"

"A couple of years." They walked through a set of opened double doors. There was a gentle hum of activity in the air. They walked past an empty cafeteria and then a recreational area with a couple of pool tables set up. Two trainees had set up a computer console and were playing a video game. Neither of them even glanced up as they walked through.

"My school wasn't anything like this," Lizzie mused, trying to sort out all of the shifter scents she was picking up at once. "I mean I didn't go to school with shifters."

"You went to a human school?"

"Yes." Lizzie nodded. "I can count my interactions with other shifters on my hand."

"Sometimes that doesn't matter. I was always by myself because of the animal I shifted into. I wanted to be an agent but was viewed as weak because I wasn't a traditional predator." Aubrey blushed. "Sorry, I guess I'm holding onto a grudge."

"I understand." And the thing was, she did. "I shift into a fennec fox."

Aubrey came to an abrupt stop and grabbed Lizzie's arm. "You mean the little foxes with big ears and large eyes. Those are adorable."

"The very same."

"You know we're not the problem. You'd think a supernatural world with hundreds, if not thousands, of different branches would be more accepting."

And there it was again. The acceptance in the other woman's eyes. She didn't judge her for her animal. That would change if she figured out why Lizzie was there. Aubrey gave her the brief tour, and then they ended up in the library. A man sat behind one of the desks and got to his feet as soon as he spied them. He looked like he was in his sixties. His grey beard was trimmed, and he wore tweed trousers, a white shirt, and a waistcoat. He had a slim built and moved with an ease that every shifter possessed.

"Ms. Taylor, I thought you were on leave."

"Good morning, Anthony. I left some of my work on my desk."

"You're supposed to take time off. It's procedure. " He crossed his arms. There was something regal about the way he held himself. A bird shifter?

Aubrey glanced at Lizzie then glared at Anthony. "Thanks for sharing that with my friend."

The man didn't look even slightly apologetic. "Did you even tell Jackson?"

The atmosphere in the room changed. The hairs on the back of Lizzie's neck stood on end. Energy came off Aubrey in waves. She looked pissed. "I said I would."

"And did you?" They glared at each other; the stalemate was awkward as hell.

Lizzie coughed and stepped forward, offering her hand to the man. "I'm Lizzie. I promise I'll keep an eye on her. All she needs to do is collect a few things, and I'll make sure she gets home again." Then she placed her hand on her chest. "You have my word."

The man wrinkled his nose, and then some of the

tension left him. He pulled Aubrey into a gentle hug. "Jackson will kill all of us if something happens to you. You know that, little mouse. I've got to see the boss lady." He stepped away and glared at Lizzie. "I'm holding you to your word." Then without even a backward glance, he disappeared between the stacks.

There was a moment of silence, and then Aubrey laughed. "He's being dramatic. I didn't fall. I tripped. It's taken me a while to get used to the pregnant belly. I'm twenty-six weeks pregnant, but I feel huge."

"You're beautiful. I still intend to get you home in one piece. I think Anthony would cause me some serious harm if I didn't," Lizzie joked. She wasn't much of a fighter but never needed to be before. Even so, she was sure she could handle the odd man.

"Anthony's a pussycat," Aubrey told her as she walked into one of the offices. "Well, he's a bird." Lizzie stayed behind, making herself look busy by flicking through a book. But she watched what Aubrey did out of the corner of her eye.

Aubrey moved a painting to the side and twisted a dial. Lizzie was too far away to make out the precise order, but seeing the old-school safe did ease some of the tension that had coiled in the pit of her stomach like a snake.

My favorite kind of safe.

Aubrey pulled a book out of it.

Was that the Bathory book Lizzie was looking for?

Then Aubrey took out her phone, snapped some photos of pages, then returned the book to the safe. Lizzie moved along, looking at the next row of books while Aubrey closed her safe and returned the painting.

When Aubrey returned to Lizzie's side, she had three folders in her hands, and her phone was nowhere to be seen. Lizzie assumed she must have slipped it into her handbag.

"Is that what you needed?" Lizzie asked as she spotted an open window across the room. She casually made her way over to it, peeking her head out and using the opportunity to drop her black bag down into the bushes. Then she turned back to Aubrey. "Do you want me to close this?"

"Sure. Anthony must have opened it." Aubrey looked at Lizzie closely, and Lizzie briefly wondered if Aubrey had seen what she'd done. If she had, she decided to change the topic. "Yeah, I got what I needed. What time is your meeting with Alyce? Is she expecting you soon? I don't want to leave you, but this short excursion has already left me ready for a nap."

"Oh, that's fine, no worries! But I promised I'd see to it that you got home safely."

"But your meeting with Alyce?"

Lizzie waved her hand, brushing away the worries. "I don't have a formal meeting time with her. She knows I'm heading here and told me to stop in whenever I'm around. I can afford to see you back to your house and then call one of those ride-share things to bring me back."

Aubrey nodded slowly, and Lizzie thought the mouse shifter was thinking the same thing she was: *Are you just finding an excuse to see Neil?*

"Ah, okay."

At least now, Lizzie had a pretty good idea of where the book was. It was a starting point. She could be wrong and could find that the item in the safe was nothing to do with Bathory, but at least, at that point, she'd have scouted FUCN'A for the next lead.

She'd come back that night and break into the Academy. She saw some points of interest in the library. She could go in through one of the windows, crack the safe, and get out with nobody the wiser.

"You want to tell me more about Neil?" She brought up the topic she knew the mouse must be dying to talk about, hoping it would distract her away from talking more about her non-existent meeting with Alyce.

"Why do you say that?" Aubrey put the folders into her satchel.

"You're his friend. I'm assuming you're going to try and sell me on the idea of us being mates. To try and get me to stay."

They walked back the way they had come. "I wouldn't do that to you." She sighed. "Neil is a good guy. He didn't think he'd ever meet his mate."

"What happens if I don't believe in the mating bond?"

The other woman bit her bottom lip and frowned. "It doesn't matter. It's true. It's like a siren's call; you can't ignore him. I've never known anyone to ignore it, either. I imagine it's not a pleasant experience fighting against the needs of your animal."

That was the last thing Lizzie needed to hear, but she respected Aubrey's honesty. "It's complicated."

"I'm sure the two of you will figure it out."

Lizzie didn't agree. By tomorrow she would be out of the town and far away from the man who wanted a future with her.

CHAPTER ELEVEN

Engine grease covered Neil's forearms. There was something peaceful about working on a motorcycle. For the first time since meeting Lizzie, his mind was clear and focused.

It helped that Jackson made sure that there was a steady stream of drinks, which Neil appreciated even if he didn't get drunk. They talked about work and reminisced about past assignments.

"I can't believe you're going to give all of it up. It doesn't feel that long ago that you were going from country to country in a smart suit, rubbing elbows with the richest and most important people in the world."

"If I remember correctly, I didn't miss the job when I had time off."

"It's just going to be strange." Neil sat down and rolled the bottle of chilled beer between his hands.

Jackson was still hunched over the motorcycle. "I'm going to be a dad. That's the most important thing in my life right now. I grew up without a dad. And my job is ten times more dangerous. I got shot in the ass. If I'd been a fraction slower, Layla would have taken out my lower spine. I don't want my son to go through that." He straightened and rubbed the back of his hand against his forehead. He left a black streak.

"I just can't see you as a teacher."

Jackson chuckled. "Okay, teaching isn't my strong suit, but there were some subjects I excelled in. I'm sure it'll be fine."

"Mister Holt." Neil tried to picture his friend in front of some fresh recruits.

"I'm pretty sure I'll still go by Jackson."

"I just can't get my head around it."

Jackson sat next to him and picked up his bottle. "You want to talk about her? I mean I don't mind sitting around chatting, but it looks like you're on a time limit. You want to have some advice?"

"I'm sure there's nothing you can tell me that's going to help. Lizzie is headstrong. If she doesn't accept the mating bond, there's nothing I can do about it." His life would have been simpler if he could just throw her over his shoulder, caveman style, and hold her prisoner until she accepted him. He was quite sure that Lizzie wouldn't appreciate the strong-arm tactic.

"You could try approaching it like a normal human being. You said that she was raised by humans, which means whatever insane connection you guys share, it's very new to her. She didn't have parents who were mates. She didn't have friends who were mates. She won't be ruled by her animal's needs. You need to take her out on a proper date and leave a good enough impression that when she returns to her own country, you won't be far from her thoughts."

"You've been watching a lot of daytime TV?"

"Aubrey has a selection of self-help books. Sometimes I get bored." He took a deep pull on his bottle. "It's rubbish, but there's some interesting stuff in them."

"And what if she says no?"

Jackson shrugged. "Then she says no. This is about both of you, not just you. She'll come around, or she won't. She won't be able to ignore the call for long."

"Do you think she's having fun with Aubrey right now?"

"I hope so. Aubrey doesn't have many friends. It would be nice if our mates became pals."

It hadn't been his idea for the mouse shifter to take his mate out for the day. Lizzie had shown interest in going to the Academy, and Aubrey had to pop in for work. She might have been a small woman, with an animal that was viewed as prey, but Aubrey was fierce with a temper to match. Only an idiot went against a pregnant woman when she set her mind to something.

"How's Cassandra handling the fact you've got me as the godparent if something happens to the both of you?" Neil asked, knowing that while Jackson's mother had a soft spot for him, she'd draw the line at a wolf raising her grand-lion cub.

"In all honesty, she figured you would say no."

"And you haven't told her I said yes?"

His best friend shook his head. "Not yet. This is her first grandchild. She's excited."

"Are you sure you want me to be the godfather? I

mean, I travel all over the world, and I'm never in one country long enough to make permanent connections. I'm not the best choice."

"Neil, you are the only choice. I know that you'd do right by my kid. That you'd keep mine and Aubrey's memory alive for them. That you'd tell them about where they came from, without any of the overbearing-control parenting that Cassandra would give them."

Neil's heart went tight in his chest, and his eyes burned. No, he wasn't going to burst into tears in front of his oldest friend. Immense pride came from his wolf. As a lone wolf with no pack, he had wanted those connections, even if he feared them. That was what he feared the most when he thought about Lizzie not accepting their bond. His feelings were so intense. Could he really just end up destined to be alone?

"You need some tissues?"

"Shut up." He pushed Jackson's shoulder. "Do you think they'll be back by now?"

"Aubrey said it was just a quick visit."

Neil heard a door opening behind them. Someone had just arrived home. The kitchen windows were open, and he caught a familiar scent. Jackson frowned and stood. "You know who that is?"

"It's her." He caught sight of Aubrey through the kitchen window and then a flash of familiar white hair before the back door opened and the women walked into the garden. The tightness in his chest eased at the sight of her. Her cheeks were flushed, and those amber eyes rooted him to the spot.

Then Neil noticed that Lizzie had one arm around Aubrey's waist, helping support her weight.

Jackson had already rushed to his mate's side. "What happened?" He knelt next to her, looking up at her.

"I'm fine."

"She started to feel a little dizzy, and after her fall, I didn't want to chance it."

Aubrey turned to look at Lizzie in shock, her mouth falling open. "You big mouth."

"And this isn't the first time either. She fell over at work, and that's why they sent her home on leave." Lizzie turned from Jackson and looked at Aubrey, pointing an accusatory finger. "Stop looking at me like that. He's your mate, and you need to tell him. Besides, it's not like you know where I live, so what do I care if you try to threaten me?"

Lizzie laughed and easily bounced away as Aubrey took a playful swing at her.

"Is she okay?" Neil asked as Jackson rushed his mate into their house, insisting on her putting her feet up.

"She says it's normal to have her balance off while pregnant." Lizzie shrugged. "But apparently she's been sent home until after her maternity leave because they don't want librarians falling over on the job."

They followed the two into the house, where they saw Aubrey on the couch, Jackson sitting next to her, holding both of her hands in his.

"We need to go see the doctor."

The mouse shifter shook her head. "The baby's fine. Still moving around like he's playing on a trampoline."

"And that's great news, but I'm worried about you. I'm sorry, guys. We're going to see Doctor Jenkins."

Aubrey groaned. "You mean the one who lives in Vancouver?"

"The very same. Only the best for my family."

"How about I promise to stay off my feet?" Aubrey went to stand, but Jackson beat her to it. He scooped his mate up into his arms.

"Lock up after us?" he asked as he moved to the front door.

"At least let me pack!"

AUBREY MANAGED TO GET JACKSON TO LET HER PACK A FEW things, and that meant telling him what she wanted so he'd pack it, as he wasn't allowing her to stand.

When they were finally off, Neil waved until the car vanished down the road. Then he returned inside to face Lizzie.

"I better go."

He grabbed her hand as she started to walk from him. "Have you had anything to eat yet?"

"Aubrey took me to the FUCN'A cafeteria when we first got there."

He wasn't sure if it was a lie or not, but her stomach rumbled at the topic of food, and he knew she was hungry.

"Come to the Hub with me. It's a great little bar. The owner, Bear, knows how to set an atmosphere almost as well as he cooks."

"I really don't think we should."

"Come on. Do me a favor. I don't want to cook all alone here, and I don't want to go out in public and eat alone either. Have pity on a sad lonely wolf."

Her mouth twisted as she considered it.

"Their burgers are awesome," he teased. "You really can't return home from Canada without being able to brag about our fantastic cuisine."

He still hadn't let go of her wrist, and without even thinking, he ran his thumb over the soft skin. She looked down at her wrist and then back up at him. She raised her eyebrow, and he let her go.

"Nothing else is going to happen between us. You understand that, don't you?"

His heart sank at her words. She still fought the mating bond, but he would take whatever she was willing to give him. "Whatever you want."

"Then let's go."

CHAPTER TWELVE

SHE HADN'T BEEN ABLE TO TELL HIM NO. THERE WAS ALSO A tiny part of her that hadn't *wanted* to say it either.

Besides, it wasn't like she could tell him that she had plans. *I'm sorry, Neil. I need to break into the Academy tonight. How about a rain check?*

The bar was busy, full of a mixture of shifters and humans. She had never been around a mixture like this, all in one place. Some of them played pool, and others sat at tables, eating their food. Lizzie's stomach rumbled.

Neil chuckled next to her, and her face went hot. Had he heard that?

"Come on. Let's grab a table."

They found a table near the back. Neil raised his hand, catching the attention of the waitress. "Two of your finest. And let Bear know that I said hello."

"Coming up. You want the usual?"

"You got any preferences for what you have on a burger?" Neil asked Lizzie, and she shook her head. "Two of the same. Same drinks as well."

Lizzie noticed that every pair of shifter eyes had moved to look at Neil at least once. It was like she was hanging out with a local celebrity. Another reason they wouldn't work. Lizzie had never liked being the center of attention.

"You come here a lot?"

"Since Jackson started frequenting the area, yeah." He sighed and ran his hand through his hair. "I can't believe he's not going to be my partner anymore."

"He's not?" To her surprise, she felt bad for him. In the short amount of time she'd known him, there was one thing he'd made clear: Jackson was his best friend, brother, and agent partner. What would Neil do without him?

What would Neil do without *her?*

LIZZIE TOOK A BITE OF HER MONSTER OF A BURGER. THE cheese melted down the side, and the lettuce still had a crunch to it. She tried to stop the moan, but as soon as she swallowed, she couldn't help herself.

"This is so good. Oh my goddess." She took another bite and noticed Neil was watching her. The heat in his eyes was hard to miss. He hadn't touched his yet. "What?"

"It shouldn't be sexy to watch you eat, but your sweet moan went straight to my cock. I was doing so well keeping it under control until then."

"I'm sorry?"

"It's not your fault. The burgers *are* damn good." He squashed his burger down with the palm of his hand then took a bite himself. The moan that came from him had a similar effect on her, but unlike him, she didn't mention it. She just squeezed her thighs together.

"Are you going to finish your story?" She prompted him to pick up where he'd left off.

"The prank of 2009? Let's just say the chickens lived out the rest of their days on a farm. What about you? What's the craziest thing you've ever done?"

"Coming to a new country by myself ranks pretty high."

"And before that?"

"My life isn't very interesting."

Neil frowned, and she realized she had lied without even thinking about it.

Coming up with something, she said, "I had a teacher, Ms. Kilburn. She taught science and spent her weekends fishing. I don't know if you do it here, but we had to dissect a frog in one of her classes. I didn't have a problem, but Amanda, my sister, did. She hadn't wanted to do it. She was so upset, but Ms. Kilburn wasn't interested in what she saw as excuses."

"Some teachers are mean."

She had some of her drink, bourbon on the rocks, enjoying the warm glow it left in her belly. "That's true. Anyway, I didn't like the fact she had made my little sister cry. In her office she had a taxidermy fish mounted, the largest one she ever caught. I snuck into her office and replaced it. Have you ever seen the singing bass?" He shook his head. "It had sensor detection, and when it's activated, it starts to sing. We heard the screams from the other side of the school."

"That's pretty ballsy."

They finished their meals, and Neil went up to the counter to pay. Now was the time. She needed to make excuses and get the hell out of Dodge. He offered his hand, and Lizzie took it; he laced their fingers together. It had been the perfect date. If he wasn't who he was and she wasn't a thief, they would have been perfect together. "Let me walk you back to the inn?"

"Okay."

His phone chimed, and he pulled it out of his pocket, explaining, "It's Jackson."

"Is Aubrey going to be okay?"

"Jackson was just being cautious. There's a significant difference between their animals and human sides, and Jackson's worried it'll play havoc on her body."

"Can that happen?"

"In all honesty, I don't have a clue." They continued to walk down the street, through the puddles of light created by the few streetlights. "Aubrey has always been self-sufficed. At the start of their relationship, his mother hadn't approved. She had wanted to keep the bloodline pure and didn't keep her dislike of Aubrey a secret."

"What changed?"

"Aubrey's smart. She was brought in by the FUC to help them decipher a book, but it made her a target to the group who wanted it to begin with. She ended up saving Cassandra's life and claiming Jackson as her mate."

The words sank in, and Lizzie wondered, was the Broker behind targeting Aubrey? Lizzie wanted to ask but couldn't think of a natural way to drop in the nickname of the man who was blackmailing her.

"What did you think of Bear's place?" Neil asked.

"The food was incredible."

"And the company?"

Lizzie stopped in her tracks. Neil turned to face her. The way his thumb ghosted over her skin made her shiver.

She looked up at him.

"I'm sorry. I shouldn't have mentioned that. I'm trying to make this a normal—"

She didn't even let him finish his sentence. Instead, she stepped into his personal space and raised onto her tiptoes, kissing him. It was a terrible idea. She knew that, but that didn't stop her. He tugged her until her body was pressed against his, and he held her in place with his arm around her waist.

After a few minutes, he pulled away, breathing heavily. "Not that I'm complaining, but what was that for?"

"Carpe diem, I suppose. I'm leaving soon. That's not going to change. I have my whole life in London. But that doesn't mean that you weren't right about my feelings."

His lips crashed against hers. They were in the middle of a deserted street, but she didn't care. She put her arms around his neck, moaning as she played with the strands of hair at the base of his skull.

He trailed a path of kisses from her mouth to the curve of her neck. "If you're still sure that you want to leave, I won't stop you. Just promise me you'll take my number and call me if you change your mind?"

She nodded, even if she knew she wouldn't change her mind. "What should we do now?"

"How about we go for a run? I know a good spot."

She smiled. "That sounds like a brilliant idea." She didn't know when she would get the chance again to run with her mate.

CHAPTER THIRTEEN

THERE WASN'T A PART OF THAT LITTLE TOWN THAT NEIL hadn't explored. There was a grove of trees near the Academy where the cadets did night-time exercises, starting at one end of the trees and running. Whoever reached the other side won. He hoped there were no exercises that night, because, even in the dark, it was a beautiful spot.

The moonlight came in through the trees, and the shadows seemed endless. Lizzie frowned as she looked at the natural obstacle course.

"What is this place?"

Neil pulled his T-shirt over his head and dropped it onto the ground. "One of the training grounds." He started to unbuckle his jeans. He loved the way she looked at him. The heated glances told him everything he needed to know. He pushed his jeans over his hips and kicked them in the same direction as the T-shirt.

"You don't like wearing clothes, do you?" she teased.

He smirked as he approached her. She didn't resist as

he started to take her clothes off. "I like it when you don't wear them much more."

She stripped, and when she was naked, he dropped to his knees and brushed a kiss against her stomach.

"Neil..."

"Just give me a moment. How good are you at keeping your balance?"

"Pretty good, why?"

He raised her leg, placing her foot over his shoulder. "Let's see if we can manage this without you falling over." She wobbled, but he placed one hand on the small of her back and the other on the back of her thigh. She laughed, but that sound vanished as he buried his face between her thighs. It wasn't a good angle, but it had less to do with getting her off than teasing her. Also, he'd been craving another taste. When he finished, she was a quivering mess who'd managed to keep her balance. He pulled away from her, and she groaned.

"That's unfair." She reached for him, but he moved out of the grasp. "What are you doing?"

"You're going to have to catch me." He took off in a run and let the change sweep over him. It wasn't an easy transition while he was running, but it was doable. He darted for the trees and kept low to the ground. They played the same game they had on the field, but he knew this would be a bigger challenge for her. All the scents were different here. The presence of others lingered on the equipment. They were faint but still recognizable to someone with keen shifter senses and still enough to disguise Neil's scent.

He didn't want her to sniff him out or race him,

though. He wanted her to have to use their mating bond to find him. The more time they spent together, the harder it was to ignore. He knew she felt it too, and there had been moments when he'd been sure she wanted to give up the fight.

He moved through holes created by fallen trees. There were also branches laid out to mask holes in the ground. Traps. None of them were lethal, but he noticed them all and made sure to miss each one. He wondered how far back she was. His wolf wanted to turn back and find her, to make the chase a little easier.

Neil ignored his wolf. *If we make it too easy, she won't try hard to find us. We need her to use the bond to try and find us. The sooner she accepts who we are to her, the sooner we'll feel whole. I promise.*

Neil went deeper into the forest. There was a small lake that ran through it. There were plenty of places to hide there and mask his scent.

Our mate.

Ours.

Lizzie watched Neil run off, shifting into his wolf as he did.

She wanted to stay more than she wanted her next breath. Neil's plan sounded perfect, and the desire to give chase was overwhelming. To feel the grass and fallen twigs underneath her paws, to hunt. But she stopped herself from giving in.

There wasn't going to be a more perfect time than this to slip away and get her job done.

Neil was distracted. He would hide in the woods waiting for her. While she could be in the Academy, searching for that book. The change swept over her, and she landed on all fours. She ignored the bite of pain. The flare of panic. Her fox wanted to go after Neil, and not for the first time, the two sides of her personality were at war with each other.

Let's go after him.

No. She pushed that word at her fox. *Think of Amanda. She's our family. We need to do what we came here to do.*

She ran toward the building. It wasn't easy figuring out where the library was from outside. She retraced her steps in her head. Bright beams of light came from around the corner, and she wriggled down in the undergrowth. Security guards.

"Did you catch the game last night?"

"I wish I hadn't," the other groaned. "The Oilers were robbed."

Lizzie tuned out their conversation. She had to reorient herself. The course Neil had taken them to had been at the back of the Academy, but she'd entered with Aubrey in the front.

From the front, they'd walked down a corridor, up a flight of stairs, through a common room. The library had been on the left, meaning Lizzie's right from her new position. When the coast was clear, she darted forward, first going to the place where she'd stashed her bag and then to the building without seeing anyone else. She'd packed light, but the added weight was still a struggle for her small form.

Most of the windows were dark. She hoped that meant all the classrooms were empty. At least, the ones on these floors. As she understood it, the night-time classes for the nocturnal shifters were mostly held in the classroom in the floors underground.

She shifted back into her human form and got dressed in black shorts and a sports bra from her little bag before peering into the window. There had to be a hundred cameras in the building and even a few set up outside, in places she couldn't see. She figured that the figure of a woman would alarm any guards less than a fennec fox running around. At least in her human form, she could look like a cadet who was heading to the cafeteria or one of the night classes.

She picked up a large rock in case she needed it but found the door was unlocked. She assumed the Academy must stay unlocked at all times since they offered classes round the clock. She pocketed the rock and headed inside, through the silent hallways.

The library was another story. Locked up tight, with posted hours explaining that nocturnal students could come for early hours at four a.m. Lizzie palmed the rock she'd brought and smashed it right next to the latch of the library door. The noise was loud in the dead of night. She had a couple of minutes if the guards had heard it. She slipped the rock back into the bag and pulled on her gloves. With the utmost care, she maneuvered her hand into the gap, minding the sharp pieces of glass that jagged inwards and unlatched the lock. Then she pushed the door open and walked inside.

Aubrey's office, on the other hand, was unlocked. Lizzie entered, seeing everything in its place, how Aubrey had left it.

They trusted you. Her fox's voice came out of nowhere, her voice accusing.

Shut up.

He'll never forgive us.

We'll survive. But Amanda won't if we fail her.

She made her way around Aubrey's desk. Even if she was the only one in the room, she kept crouched. The office was far away from the main door, but she couldn't risk anyone seeing her by accident. She lifted the painting off the wall and pressed her ear against the safe.

Left, right, right, left, left, right.

She held her breath as she turned the dial and pulled. The safe swung open, and she reached inside. The book was lighter than she thought it would be, but she didn't have any time to worry or question it. Instead, she closed the safe, turned the dial, and replaced the frame.

A beam of light cut through the darkness of the library. Her heart skipped a beat, and she dashed for the window. It would have been so easy for her to panic, to slam the window open and jump for her escape, but years of experience helped to push the urge away. She slowly and cautiously opened the window, climbed through it, and then carefully lowered the window, not making a single sound.

Then she shimmied down the drain pipe, going from the second floor to the ground. She pulled out a larger bag from her pouch and put the book inside. It would be a struggle to carry it in her fox form, so she would get as far away from the Academy as she could first.

She put the bag on and ran back for the trees.

When she was a safe distance away, she slipped out of her clothes and shoved them into the bag, which was almost as large as her fox but had been specially made for her to wear while in fur.

Then she shifted back into her fox form. Tiredness swept over her, but she did her best to ignore it. She couldn't stop. Not even for one short nap. A thief never stayed in the area after a job. Even if they connected the security cam footage to the woman Aubrey had brought to the campus, they probably wouldn't be able to get hold of Aubrey for a few days, and even then, it didn't matter. As Lizzie had jokingly said earlier, Aubrey didn't know where she lived. She didn't even know Lizzie's last name. FUC wouldn't find her.

Just like the Broker won't find me once I vanish.

She trudged on, knowing that Neil was back there, thinking she was in the forest looking for him.

He trusted us.

She tried to shake off the feeling of guilt. She had accomplished what she had set out to do. The book was in her possession. Amanda would be safe. She'd leave in the morning and never look back.

Right. In the morning. We could still go find Neil. Leave this book with my pile of clothes where we'd taken off. Have one last night with our mate before he learns about what I've done.

She picked up the pace, returning to their pile of

clothes. She dumped off the bag and then turned back to run off in the direction she'd last seen Neil running.

Her fox body nimbler and quicker, she leaped up onto a low branch and looked around. Then she closed her eyes and let her senses spread out, like a fisherman with a net. An owl. Small forest animals. The wind in the trees. No Neil.

She caught the sound of running water and made her way toward it. That was an effective way to disrupt your scent. She had seen plenty of movies where the prisoners had gone through running water to shake off hunting dogs. She didn't know how true it was, but it was a start.

CHAPTER FOURTEEN

NEIL STAYED IN HIS HIDING SPOT, WAITING. HE HAD ENDED up half submerged in the water, his snout just above it, and right next to some stones. With his wet fur, she might mistake him for another rock. Unless, of course, she used the bond.

There was no telling if she watched him as he anticipated her making an appearance. He didn't have any concept of time in his wolf form, but even he knew she was taking her time. He fought against the urge to move and look for her. It was what she wanted, for him to break first. He closed his ears and listened.

There was the steady stream of water. There was even the sound of small animals. They kept their distance because they sensed the predators who lived there. Nobody wanted to end up as a midnight snack for someone with the munchies.

A twig snapped to his left. He stopped himself from turning, knowing that the sound of water moving would give his position away. He still couldn't sense her. In his human form, he had a narrow field of vision. His wolf didn't suffer from the same limitation. He scanned the forest from his vantage point. With her white fur, Lizzie should have been easy to see, except he couldn't see her.

She would make an impressive agent. Now that was an idea. She had never been clear about what she did for a living, but if Jackson wanted to leave, Neil needed a new partner. He filed away the thought. It was too hopeful. She'd been clear she was going home.

A branch cracked above him, and he glanced up as a ball of white fur cannonballed toward him. He didn't have time to move out of the way, so he took the hit. She landed on his back, and they both went under the water. Neil broke back through the surface first. He looked around for Lizzie, spotted her, and lurched forward, nipping the back of her neck, and lifted her out of the water. She shrugged, making adorable yipping noise of displeasure. Neil walked them out of the icy water, dropped her to the ground, and shook his body. Droplets went flying in every direction as Lizzie did the same.

Neil didn't bother to shift back into his human form. He led her to some grass. There was a scattering of leaves, and he walked in a circle before he collapsed to the ground. Lizzie curled up next to him. Her yawn didn't escape his notice. It had been a long couple of days. The need to lose himself in her body would have to wait till the morning. She needed to rest, and he wanted the same thing. At that moment, their connection didn't have anything to do with sex.

HE WOKE UP TO HAVE A PLEASANT WEIGHT ACROSS HIS HIPS and a warm wet heat rubbing against his cock. It was still dark, but the sky had started to lighten. He didn't know when his body had shifted back into his human form, but he didn't care. All he cared about was the woman saddling him. Beautiful and fierce. He'd been lucky the goddess had blessed him with a mate like her. Her hair had dried in wild curls, and her eyelids were heavy, her amber irises drowned out by her pitch-black pupils. He opened his mouth to say something, but she pressed her fingers against his lips. He opened for her, and she pushed her fingers into his mouth.

The taste of her delicious nectar exploded on his tongue, and he groaned. Had she been playing with herself? The thought of her getting herself off without him didn't sit right. He wanted to be the one to get her off. He could dedicate a substantial amount of his time to bringing her blinding pleasure. It wouldn't be a hardship. She smiled wickedly at him and continued to roll her hips. It was a maddening pace. He needed to be inside of her, but she was the one controlling the encounter, controlling him. Every time he thought he might slip inside, she pulled away. He continued to suck on her fingers until they were completely clear. He tried to move his hands to her waist, but she slapped them away and shook her head.

Ours.

All ours.

The fact he didn't have an ounce of control over the situation thrilled him in a way he didn't think was possible.

Let her use our body how she feels fit. We are hers.

He gripped the ground on either side of him and held on tight. They might have used words, but he wanted the message to be clear. He was giving himself to her. She leaned forward, her lips ghosting over his.

"Good boy," she whispered. Then she reached between them, and with one hand, she directed him to her entry. She lowered, taking an inch before lifting off. Neil went cross-eyed at the sweet torture. Then she did it again. This time she went just a bit farther as his hips bucked, sinking another inch inside of her before she removed him. Sweat glistened across her body, her nipples were like tiny pebbles, and he wanted to taste them, to make them harder. He groaned as he looked down the line of their joined bodies and saw his cock glistening with her juices. Fuck, that was hot.

Her hand went back to the base of his cock. It wouldn't take much for him to get off, and he gritted his teeth, determined he wouldn't explode until she allowed him. She continued her torture as the sun broke over the horizon. A warm glow appeared across her body, and not for the first time, he noticed how beautiful she was. In the morning light, she looked like the incredible supernatural creature she was.

She took four inches inside of her and shuddered. Neil was above average. There were about another three inches left to fill her, to stretch her to breaking point. How long did she plan on doing this? How much more could he take before he flipped her onto her back and pushed inside of her? She hovered over him, her hand on his chest. The flush on her face went down to her chest.

She trembled at the strain. This had to be affecting her as much as him.

Then she sank the rest of the way. She cried out, and the waking birds scattered. Neil groaned, the heat of her sex like a tight hug.

"Take what you want from me, sweetheart."

"You are mine." She moaned the words as she started to rise and fall.

"All yours," Neil grunted in agreement. The weight on his heart lifted. This was the first time she'd admitted her feelings. Sure, it wasn't a declaration of love, but it was better than the uncertainty.

"Fuck me, love." The pressure built at the bottom of his spine. "I'm not going to last long after all of that."

She picked up her pace, and he loosened his grip on the grass. He reached between them and flicked the bundle of nerves. When she tumbled into oblivion, he went right off the proverbial cliff with her.

***

AFTER THEIR ESCAPADES NEAR DAWN, NEIL WAS STILL asleep when Lizzie woke up. She rolled away from him, being careful not to wake him. She should have left in the middle of the night. He'd been dead to the world and in his human form. She hadn't been able to help herself.

You are mine.

Her own words echoed in her mind. She got to her feet and took one last look at him. His arm was half slung over his face, and the rest of him was deliciously bare. There was no telling how long she had before he woke.

The last couple of days had consisted of time and not having enough of it. She closed her eyes and sniffed the air. Nothing. They were the only two in the forest.

Lizzie made her way back to where they had left their clothes and got dressed. Her body ached in the best possible way. She was going to miss this. She was going to miss him.

She slipped her boots on and checked on the bag. The book and the burner phone were still there.

There was only one number saved in the directory, and as she continued to walk, she tapped the number.

"Hello?" The quick response surprised her.

"I've got it."

For a few seconds, the phone was silent in her hand. "You got the book?" He sounded surprised, and Lizzie did her best to ignore the stab of annoyance.

"Yes. I'm calling for extraction."

"You can't get out of Canada by yourself?"

Lizzie gritted her teeth. "In the best-case scenario, I'd have a couple of hours before they noticed the book's missing. Hell, I might even have a couple of days since it looks like Aubrey's the only one who can access it, but that's not a risk I'm willing to take. If you want the bloody book, come get it!" she snapped. She was leaving the man she had feelings for. There was a chance they would never see each other again, and if they did, it would be because Neil was hunting her. She had the right to be pissed.

"I'd watch my tone if I were you." All the surprise had disappeared from his voice. The change was scary. "Your sister isn't out of the woods until I have that book in my hands."

"The sooner you send someone, the sooner you'll have it. Where do you want to meet?"

"There's an abandoned airstrip, McDonnell's, about ten miles out from where your phone is pinging off the towers. Be there in two hours."

The phone went dead in her head. She fought against the urge to throw it. This one act was going to burn all the bridges that had been forged in such a short amount of time. Her eyes burned, but she took a deep breath. She wasn't going to cry. She slipped the phone into her back pocket and started the walk. Tears trickled down her cheeks, and she angrily wiped them away.

This is for the best. There was no way she could stay. She had betrayed them. They wouldn't understand, and Neil would think this had been her plan all along. It was time to go back to her old life, for however long she had it.

CHAPTER FIFTEEN

Something's wrong. Wake up. Neil opened his eyes. The morning sunlight came through the canopy of trees, and he groaned, shielding his eyes. He yawned as he sat up, and then he remembered the words from his wolf. Something was wrong. Panic surged through him, and he was on his feet and searching for her.

"Lizzie?!"

She didn't answer him. He closed his eyes and let his wolf come to the surface. With deliberate intent, he cast out his senses. The technique worked comparably to a wolf stalking its prey. He listened for the slightest bit of movement, and he tried to catch a whiff of her scent. There wasn't any. Wherever his mate was, it wasn't in the immediate area. He took off in a run to where their clothes had been discarded the night before. Hers were gone.

Is she going to leave without even saying goodbye?

Last night had felt like a goodbye. Their time together had always been explosive, but the way she had taken control of the situation, how she had whispered the words, claiming him... That could have been her way of saying goodbye. Neil shook his head. The best he could do was let her leave. It didn't matter what he had hoped for. She had made up her mind. One last night together hadn't changed that. He pulled his clothes on. Her scent still lingered. Though it was faint, he knew that scent as well as his own. The bundle of clothes had been the last place she had been before she ran.

He was torn. On one hand, he knew she wanted him to let her go. It was what she wanted. On the other hand, she had left without even saying goodbye. Didn't he deserve that much at least? How could she leave, like she wasn't taking a part of him with her? All he knew with any certainty was he would regret just letting her leave. He took off in the direction her scent was strongest. He didn't know how much of a lead she had on him, but since she was moving away from Academy and toward the town, she might have been heading to the B&B to collect her things. Had she already arranged transport out?

WITH ENOUGH FORCE TO CRACK THE WOOD, HE SHOVED THE door to the B&B open. A woman, Martine, sat behind the counter and glanced up in shock, her hand to her chest. It would just be his luck if he gave someone a heart attack in his rush.

"Is Lizzie Adams still here?"

The woman frowned. "You burst in here without even an apology for your manners or lack of them?"

"I'm sorry. Please, is Lizzie here?"

"I'm afraid not. She left half an hour ago, mighty upset. Did you lovebirds have an argument?"

She'd been crying? "No, but I need to find her before she leaves town. Did she say anything else? Maybe where she was going and how?"

The woman tapped her pencil onto the table in front of her. "She did ask where the McDonnell's airstrip was. That was odd. I told her it's been out of commission since the eighties."

Why would she go there? "Thanks for your help." He ran back outside and in the direction of the airstrip. He drew curious stares as he ran. There was no way he could be mistaken for an early morning runner in his jeans and T-shirt.

The elderly woman had been right. McDonnell's had been decommissioned when the FUC decided they wanted a place for planes to land closer to the town. Neil didn't know what happened there now. As far as he was aware, it was just an empty field. Had she managed to arrange for transport to leave the town? She hadn't talked much about her work, but he figured she earned a lot of money for it. Traveling from the UK to Canada wasn't cheap. He kept running. It would have been quicker in his wolf form, but he didn't fancy taking off his clothes as he walked up Main Street. There was every chance she was already gone, but he couldn't think like that. He had to at least try.

With the town far behind him, he noticed the old wooden shack. Back in the day, it had been used by farmers or people earning money working as airplane taxis. Now it was overgrown, and weeds had taken over the area a long time ago. It wouldn't be safe for a plane to land. With his heart in his throat, he ran for the wooden shack. The building had seen better days, but it was still in one piece.

"Lizzie, are you here!" He shouted out for her, moving around the building, trying to find the door.

"Neil?" She appeared from around the other side, her expression a mixture of guilt and surprise. "How did you find me?"

He ignored her and pulled her into a tight embrace. "I can't believe you were just going to leave without saying goodbye." He didn't let her go. The hour or so they'd been apart had been the longest of his life. He had thought she was gone.

She tried to pull away. "Neil, let go of me."

"In a minute." He brushed a kiss against the top of her head. Some of the tension left her, and then she got her hands between them and pushed.

"You've got to go." She looked away from him, at the sky and then the road that led up to the airstrip.

"Don't you want to say goodbye?"

"Neil, we don't have time for this. You've got to hide."

And that was when it hit him. She was scared. The emotion was bitter in the air. If he hadn't been getting up close and personal with her, he might have missed it. "Why are you scared?"

"Why did you come after me?" She grabbed his arm

and pulled him toward the shack. "The last few days have been perfect. Last night couldn't have been a better good-bye. Why are you ruining it?"

"Why are you being a coward?" He yanked his arm free.

She stopped in surprise. "I'm trying to keep you safe." Lizzie made to grab him again, but he stepped away.

"Before who gets here? Lizzie, are you in trouble?"

They both lifted their heads at the same time. There was a helicopter in the sky, a tiny blimp in an otherwise cloudless sky. "Christ, Neil, you must hide. He'll kill you if he sees you."

A million questions raced through his head, but instead of demanding she answer any of them, he went to the shack. Lizzie's bag was on the floor, and next to it, was a black bag he hadn't seen before. He didn't know what made him pick it up, but he did, and he opened it. A familiar book came into sight. He reached inside and pulled it out. "Why do you have this? I mean, how did you even get this? Aubrey keeps it locked in a safe."

"I stole it." She glanced at the wooden floorboards. "You don't have to believe me, but he threatened to go after my human sister if I didn't help him. Her name's Amanda Adams, and she works at one of the law firms. Cooper, Bearing, and Taylor."

She spoke in a rush, her words a wild mess, but one thing was clear. She'd admitted to stealing from the Academy; his mate was a thief.

"Please give the book back to me?" she pleaded with him. Was this why she was upset? Because she was put into a situation she couldn't control? He kept studying her as the sound of the helicopter became louder. Her tear-streaked cheeks, her red eyes. It could have been an act. Was any of it true?

Our mate. Those two words came through clearly. The woman in front of them was theirs to protect. That hadn't changed. The mating bond couldn't be faked.

"We'll help you."

Her eyes widened, and she took a step back, surprised. "What?"

"We'll help you," he said again. "Let us, please."

She shook her head. "I can't. If I don't give them the book, he'll kill her."

He still held on to the book. "I won't let that happen. Do you have a phone?"

"Yes."

"Give it to me. I have a contact in London. He'll get her to safety."

She pulled a phone from the back pocket of her jeans, and without any hesitation, she handed it over to him. The time difference was a little off, but he crossed his fingers as he dialed the number he knew by heart.

"Hello?" a woman asked. "Who is this?"

"I'm sorry for calling so late, but is Gerald there?"

In the background, Neil heard another woman's voice and then a man's. "Who is this?"

"Gerald, it's me. I need your help." He gave all the information Lizzie had given him to the horse shifter. "It might be dangerous, but I'll owe you for this."

"It's fine. I'll call you when I've got her. Do you want me to call you on this number or go through the usual channels?" The helicopter was close, and Lizzie looked through the glassless window of the shack. She had her arms crossed, and she bit her bottom lip.

"Usual channels. If you can't get a hold of me, tell your point of contact something happened at the old landing strip."

"Be safe." The phone went dead in Neil's hand as he went to join Lizzie at the window. The helicopter was now close enough that Neil could make out the pilot's face. They had a couple of minutes, maybe a little more.

"We need to get out of here."

"Where are we going to go? There's half a mile between us and some coverage. They'll see us."

"Then I suggest we go now." He grabbed her hand, and they both ran out of the shack. He couldn't hear anything over the sound of the propellors, but he didn't let go of her.

CHAPTER SIXTEEN

Lizzie ran until the muscles in her legs burned. The almost rhythmic sound of the helicopter's propellors had slowed, but she didn't even dare to look back. They would be lucky. They would leave when they realized Lizzie wasn't going to hand over the book. That she wasn't alone.

Rat-tat-tat. The unmistakable sound of a gun.

Neil didn't even slow, and the line of trees was close. Even after what had happened, she couldn't believe he had trusted her. *It doesn't matter. Amanda's going to be safe. That's what matters.*

There was a hard punch-like sensation across her calf muscle, and Lizzie went down. She screamed, but without missing a beat, Neil picked her up and helped get her to the trees. They shielded behind them as he looked at her leg. Tears streamed down her face. A shifter could heal a lot of damage, but she'd never had to put that theory into practice before.

"Lizzie, look at me."

Her black jeans did a decent job at hiding the blood but not a perfect one. "Fuck." She looked up, and Neil smiled at her.

"Not right now, sweetheart. It looks like the bullet went all the way through. There were two people in the helicopter. Both are heading toward us now." He took off his shirt and tied it around the bottom of her knee.

"Any excuse to get naked."

"I don't suppose you have a gun in that bag of yours?"

She shook her head. "I don't use them. Do you have a plan?"

"It would have been a better one if I had a gun." There was another burst of bullets, and she flinched as shards of bark flew in different directions. "Stay here."

He shifted into his wolf form and moved from tree to tree. There wasn't another volley of bullets. Hadn't they seen him? Maybe they weren't worried about him. She had been the one working for their boss. Neil had told her to stay put, but the urge to keep moving wasn't an easy one to ignore.

"You must be Lizzie." She glanced up at the unfamiliar male voice. It was always difficult to gauge the correct age for shifters, so Lizzie didn't bother. He was lean, his sleeves rolled up to reveal powerful muscles. The gun in his hand was pointed at the ground. His partner was older, with grey hair at his temples and dark eyes. Even as a human, there was nothing human in those eyes. He looked like someone who killed without a second thought.

"And you're the asshole who shot me."

"You were running away."

"No, I was grabbed by an agent of FUC and dragged away. The Broker is going to be pissed when he finds out you hurt one of his assets." She bluffed for all she was worth.

The men shared a look, and the one with the gun yanked her to her feet. The pain was unbearable, and she stumbled. "Where did he go?"

"I don't know." That was the truth. If either of the men were shifters, they would know that. She wanted to look for Neil—he had to be close—but she stopped herself.

"Do you have the book?"

She nodded at the bag on the ground. "It's in there."

As the man with the black eyes bent to retrieve the book, Neil struck. He latched onto the man's exposed neck, and the man screamed. The ear-piercing sound made Lizzie's stomach twist up into knots. The other man tried to raise his gun, but Lizzie stamped down with her damaged leg, catching his foot. He lashed out with his free hand and slapped Lizzie around the face. She fell to the ground. The blinding pain made it impossible to think.

The first man had stopped screaming. The other man raised his gun again. Lizzie grabbed for the strap and pulled.

Rat-tat-tat. The shots went wide.

"Stop!" Lizzie looked up at the barrel of the gun, but he wasn't talking to her. "You take one more fucking step, and I will fill her with so many bullets you won't even recognize her."

Neil growled.

"You're going to let us leave. Do you understand me?"

It wasn't even a question, and Lizzie could see the rage

in Neil's eyes. There was no way he would be quick enough to stop the man from pulling the trigger. He nodded his head, and then his eyes flickered to her. A message? A silent promise? The man yanked her to her feet again. This time, she was ready for it, even though everything went blurry. How much blood had she lost? She held the bag close to her chest. How long did she have before the man noticed she didn't have the book?

He grabbed her around the waist. The touch repulsed her. Her inner fox howled in displeasure. She didn't know who this man was, but she sure as hell didn't want him touching her. They started to back away, and Neil growled, edging closer. Was he going to try something? *My life isn't worth yours.* She mentally pushed that message to him. *I love you, Neil.*

He faltered. Had he heard her?

If she got on that helicopter, she would be dead by morning. At least she no longer had to worry about her sister. Lizzie trusted Neil when he'd promised to keep Amanda safe.

Her kidnapper hadn't lowered his gun. If Neil tried to get to her, he'd be killed. The way the muscles were bunched in his hind legs, it looked like he was about to pounce. He wouldn't make it, at least not without a little help. She let her left arm drop and tilted her hand so he could see her palm. The man didn't notice, but Neil did.

Four, three, two, one.

On the one, she turned and pulled the strap of the gun again, making sure it wasn't pointing at her mate. The man grunted in surprise, and she managed to grab the barrel of the gun. He hadn't taken his finger off the trigger, and she managed to point the gun up into the sky as he pressed it.

He screamed as Neil bit his ankle, and he dropped the gun. There was too much going on, but he focused on dislodging Neil, the gun forgotten for a moment.

Lizzie hadn't let go. She grabbed the strap with one hand and tried to pull it off his shoulder. The man swore, but Neil hadn't let go of his ankle. Something cracked, and the man's eyes rolled back into his head as he collapsed to the ground.

Neil still hadn't let go. The man wasn't fighting back anymore, and Neil shook his head like a giant dog with a chew toy. Lizzie knelt. She knew she was still hurting but couldn't feel any pain. That would be a different story in the morning.

"Neil, you need to let him go." He looked at her, blood smeared across his snout. "I think the FUC would prefer at least one of them alive, don't you?"

He made a noise of dissatisfaction but let the leg fall to the ground. Lizzie collapsed to the ground, and Neil curled up next to her. "I'll be okay. Thanks to you." Her body was already healing the damage, but it took a lot of energy. "Maybe you should shift back and call in backup. I don't think you will be able to carry both of us."

LIZZIE WOKE UP IN A STERILE WHITE ROOM, WHICH SHE appreciated considering she thought she'd wake up in a cell. She had stolen from the Academy. She would end up on some blacklist. It was because of her connection with

Neil that she was getting treatment. But that couldn't last forever. There was an IV in her arm, and she struggled to sit up. She was the only one in the infirmary, but she must have triggered a silent alarm because a nurse had come in.

"How are you feeling?"

"Like I've been shot?"

The woman grinned at her. "If you're well enough to joke, I'm sure you'll be fine. I'll let your visitors know."

"I have visitors?" Did she mean Neil? God, she hoped so.

"I'll let them know they can come in." The nurse left, and a few seconds later, Jackson, Aubrey, and Neil walked in. Jackson carried a bouquet, and Aubrey had a bag. They were the last people Lizzie thought she would see. Didn't Neil tell them what happened? Why she had been there? How could they look so happy to see her?

Neil sat on the left side of the bed and automatically picked up her hand. Aubrey was directed to an available chair, and Jackson put the flowers onto the bedside cabinet. "What's all this?"

"We didn't know what you needed, but I packed you some fresh clothes." The mouse shifter smiled at her, one hand on her overly large belly.

"I don't understand." She looked at Neil. "Didn't you tell them what I did?"

"Lizzie…" Jackson spoke from his place just behind his mate. "You were put into an impossible situation. Would it have been easier if you had told someone about what happened? Yes, but you had no connection with the FUC and no reason to trust us. You made the right decision in the end. That's all that matters."

"What happens now?"

"Our head of security wants to talk to you, and I talked to the higher-ups at the FUC. They're interested in offering you a job."

Gods, she was glad she wasn't standing. She would worry about that snippet of information when it was just her and Neil. "And Amanda? Did they get to her in time?"

Neil squeezed her hand. "She's okay. My contact, Gerald, is going to bring her here. It's the safest place until the Broker has been put away. We haven't gotten any useful information out of his lackey yet, but it's only a matter of time."

Jackson growled, and the pair shared a look. "No one threatens our mates and gets away with it. It's long past time we found that monster and put him under the ground. Did you get a face-to-face meeting with him?"

"I saw him for about half a minute, and then I was injected with something. I never got a clear look at him."

CHAPTER SEVENTEEN

The nurse came in after an hour and shepherded Jackson and Aubrey out. Aubrey gave Lizzie a tight hug, promising to see her soon. Jackson had already informed Neil it was just a short visit. Doctor Jenkins wanted Aubrey to stay in the city just in case there was any complication. Jackson had asked if Neil could house-sit for them for a couple of days. He'd said yes.

Lizzie was going to be tied up in meetings with Alyce for a couple of days, and he would lose his mind if he didn't keep himself occupied. He knew the llama shifter. She would listen to Lizzie's story, but there was no guarantee she'd believe her.

Neil was lucky he had accumulated a lot of holiday days. After finding Lizzie, he was in no rush to get back to work.

"I thought you would all be angry with me. I thought all of you would hate me."

"It's not like you had a choice." Neil crawled onto the bed with her, and she snuggled into the crook of his arm.

"I mean I did lie to you in the beginning. I'd say we're even."

"It's not the same. You omitted that you were a FUC agent, and I omitted I was a professional thief."

"I think you should cut yourself some slack. You didn't hurt anyone, and I think I would forgive you for most things unless you squirt ketchup all over your chips. I might not be able to forgive you for that."

She nudged his ribs. "I'm glad I stayed."

"Are you sure?"

"What do you mean?"

"You can't go back to your old life. The Broker knows who you are and where you live. If you go back to your old life, he'll find you. And you've also got Amanda coming. She will want to see a friendly face since we've uprooted her entire life."

Her body went rigid but then relaxed next to him. "I know. I don't think Amanda is going to forgive me any time soon. Her job as a lawyer was her whole life. I'm responsible for her losing all of that."

"At least she's alive. That gives you both the opportunity to make peace. Anyway, I'm looking forward to meeting her."

"You are?"

"She'll be my sister-in-law. I have enough family I've lost contact with or never seen. I want to build something new, not destroy."

His mate curled up even closer to him, and he brushed a kiss against the top of her head. "You're not going to lose me. Even if I don't know if I'm going to be thrown into jail by the end of the week."

"I wouldn't worry about that too much. I talked to my bosses. If Alyce clears you, they want to offer you a job."

"What kind of job?"

He paused, running the tips of his fingers up and down her arm. "Well, it looks like my partner is giving up the life to become a dad and teacher."

"You want me to work with you?" She pulled away, and Neil let her. There wasn't much room on the bed, so she couldn't get too far away without landing on the floor in a heap. "Are you sure?"

"It was my idea. You've got a unique set of skills, and I need someone I trust to watch my back."

For a second, he thought that she was going to argue with him, but he paused the conversation to tighten his embrace, making her fall against him. "And they agreed to that?"

"I didn't give them much of a choice. You're my mate. There isn't anyone I trust more than you." He frowned. "Don't tell Jackson that; it would break his heart." He kissed her, and she made a sound of protest before melting against him.

Her body had healed from the damage caused by the gunshot wound. The reason she collapsed was because of the multiple shifts. The act had taken a toll on her body. Those would have been good enough reasons to stop, but another good reason was the door opening behind them.

The nurse coughed, and he pulled away from Lizzie, her eyes half-closed and her lips red. "We won't be having any of that."

He flashed his best smile at her, and the woman blushed. "Of course not. Sorry for getting carried away."

"That smile needs to come with a warning and shouldn't be used on a poor, old woman who's trying to do their job." She fanned herself. "You're a very lucky lady, miss."

"You won't get any argument from me on that," his mate said, her face hot against his skin.

LIZZIE COULDN'T BELIEVE WHAT WAS HAPPENING. SHE expected to be locked in a cell or at least chained to the bed. Instead, she was curled up on a hospital bed with her mate.

Ours.

She agreed with her fox. Those moments didn't happen very often; being with Neil had somehow merged the two sides of her. She had been arguing with herself for days, fighting what she felt for the dark-haired shifter. Her animal had known the truth, the one Lizzie had been too scared to face. It was insane. It shouldn't have worked in the slightest, but she fell in love with him, against all her better judgment.

"I love you. You know that, don't you?" The words said against his chest were muffled, but he must have heard them. She felt his fingers as they laced in her hair, and he moved her head, looking into her eyes.

"Say that again?"

Her face went hot, and she sympathized with the nurse. That was a potent smile. "I love you."

"I love you too." He guided her face up and kissed her. There wasn't enough space on the bed, but the masterful way he explored her mouth made her wish they could at least try something. He half shielded her body with his, and his hand went to her waist, holding her close. She remembered the first conversation they had on the plane. Lizzie still considered herself to be an independent woman. She had lived her life alone and on her own terms. Being with Neil would change that, but for the first time, the thought didn't scare her. It was time to give up a little control.

She pushed against his chest. "We've got plenty of time for that. How long am I here for?"

"They were sorting out the discharge papers, and then we can leave. We'll have a pair of agents keeping an eye on the house."

"Just in case I try to make a run for it?"

"It's just procedure. I'll take you to see Alyce in the morning."

"I did break into the Academy. If I can't prove I was blackmailed, your bosses could have me in a cell without even blinking an eye."

"Then I would get you out of it."

"You'd break the law for me?"

"Without question." He detangled himself from her embrace. "I'll go chase up those discharge papers."

There was no point thinking about tomorrow. Her sister was safe. Lizzie was with her mate. Tomorrow could wait. She would just enjoy the moment.

EPILOGUE

SIX WEEKS LATER.

LIZZIE SIGNED THE LAST FORM AND THEN SHOOK OUT HER hand. It had cramped up after the sixth, and she was sure the last one was number twelve. Her signature had become an unintelligible mess. When she was finished, she pushed the stack of papers and pen over to the legendary Miranda Brownsmith. The sabertoothed rabbit shifter smiled at her.

"Well done. Now was that so hard?"

"It feels like all of my fingers were broken and glued back on the wrong way."

Miranda laughed. She was short and dressed in a trouser suit, which didn't suit her in the slightest. She had told Lizzie she preferred summer wear, but there was a loose dress code at the Academy, and the suit was more intimidating. "Well, I could have staggered out all the forms, but where would the fun be in that?"

She got to her feet and offered her hand. Lizzie made a conscious effort to shake it with the less sore hand. "Thanks for this."

"Welcome to the team. You think signing was hard? Wait for training to start!"

LIZZIE SHIELDED HER EYES AS SHE WALKED OUT OF WANC. A probationary FUC agent. A stable job where she wouldn't have to use her abilities to break into buildings and steal things. A pang of regret hit her. She was going to miss being the boss in her life. The thrill of stealing wasn't going to be easy to get over, but she was pretty sure the rush she craved could be replaced with working with the FUC. It was a dangerous job, but at least she would be with Neil.

Speaking of Tall, Dark, and Handsome… He waved at her from his place, leaning against the car. She smiled back at him. The tension and panic at having a regular job eased at the sight of him. She was with him. That made it worthwhile. She threw herself at him when he was within arm's reach and kissed him.

He spun her around and pressed her against the car. A few of the cadets who weren't in class wolf-whistled, and she blushed. Neil moaned against her hungry mouth and pulled away.

"It's been a couple of hours. How can you kiss me like you haven't seen me for months?"

"Are you complaining? I could kiss you less."

"You wouldn't dare, would you?" He looked down at her lips, and a heat wave shot through her. "I'm not complaining. How did it go?"

"Just finished up with the last of the paperwork. How

about we leave here and I'll show you how much I missed you?"

"I'm afraid we already have plans."

"We do?"

"Jackson called. Aubrey went into labor this morning."

As soon as the words left his lips, Lizzie pressed him away. "Why didn't you say so? Get your ass into the driver's seat, buddy." She got into the car and pulled Miranda's pen out of her pocket before she damaged it. She smiled as she twisted it between her fingers.

Neil got into the car and frowned. "That's not yours, is it?"

"It's Miranda's. I'll return it when I get back."

"You better, or we'll have to add spanking to your list of punishments. "

"It's not a punishment if I enjoy it."

"Naughty girl. You ready to go be godparents?" He put the car into drive.

"Let's go."

The End.

Or is it? There are still lots of mysteries to be solved!

And there are more FUC Academy books from other authors coming your way soon!

To find out more about these books and more, visit worlds.EveLanglais.com or sign up for the EveL Worlds newsletter. If you haven't already downloaded the **free Academy intro** (written by Eve Langlais) make sure you grab it at worlds.evelanglais.com/wordpress/book/fucacademy1!

THE LION AND THE MOUSE

This mouse is about to receive the lion's share of adventure...

Aubrey Taylor dreamed of becoming an international superspy, but her parents warned that a mouse shifter wasn't meant for such risky professions. Instead, she became a librarian for the Furry United Coalition Newbie Academy, though she never dreamed she'd receive a call that would see her off on the experience of a lifetime.

Jackson Holt, lion shifter and famed FUC agent is facing a foe more powerful than any FUC enemy... his mother. She wants her alpha son to assume his position as leader of their pride, but Jackson doesn't want any of it. He wants to save the world, one FUC mission at a time.

When he swings by the academy to thank Aubrey for her assistance on a case, he inadvertently brings danger to her door. Between shots fired, jaguar assassins, and a lioness mother who will never accept her son with a mouse, Jackson has his work cut out for him.

Can this mouse remove the lion's thorn, or will she scurry back to her quiet life at the Academy?

*The Lion and the Mouse is a Furry United Coalition Newbie Academy (FUCN'A) book, set in Eve Langlais' EveL Worlds and is **available on all platforms**!*

Samantha Allard has always wanted to be a writer. She spent her teenage years reading books and scribbling notes on napkins. Now she's older, perhaps not any wiser, and getting her stories published. Young adult, steampunk or fantasy. The genre doesn't matter as long as the story is told.

She can be found in her office most days. Others she trapped at the dreaded day job.

goodreads.com/9792435.Samantha_Allard

facebook.com/samanthaallardwriter

instagram.com/samanthaallard_writer